SO-AZG-499

J 398 SIL   Child Coll   18653

Silverberg

Kitten caboodle.

Date Due

DATE DUE

Demco, Inc. 38-293

Kitten Caboodle

Kitten Caboodle

A COLLECTION OF FELINE FICTION

EDITED BY BARBARA SILVERBERG

Illustrated with drawings by T. A. Steinlen

18653

HOLT, RINEHART AND WINSTON
New York   Chicago   San Francisco

WITHDRAWN FROM
J. Eugene Smith Library
EASTERN CONN. STATE UNIVERSITY
WILLIMANTIC, CT 06226

J
398
S

Text Copyright © 1969 by Barbara Silverberg.
All rights reserved, including the right to reproduce this book or portions
thereof in any form.
Published simultaneously in Canada by Holt, Rinehart and Winston of
Canada, Limited.
SBN: 03-066220-6 Trade edition
SBN: 03-066225-7 HLE edition
Library of Congress Catalog Card Number: 69-11813
Printed in the United States of America
First Edition

4/70

ACKNOWLEDGMENTS

"Phut Phat Concentrates" by Lilian Jackson Braun. Copyright © 1963 by
Davis Publications, Inc.; first published in *Ellery Queen's Mystery Maga-
zine;* reprinted by permission of the author's agent, Blanche C. Gregory,
Inc.

"Smith" by Ann Chadwick, from *Best Cat Stories* edited by Michael Joseph,
Faber & Faber, Ltd., 1952; reprinted by permission of the author's agents,
Winant, Towers Limited.

"Dick Whittington" from "History of Sir Richard Whittington" reprinted
in *Sir Richard Whittington* by W. Besant and J. Rice, New York, G. P.
Putnam's Sons, 1881.

"The Story of Webster" from *Mulliner Nights* by P. G. Wodehouse. Copyright © 1930, 1958 by Pelham Grenville Wodehouse; reprinted by permission of the author and his agents, Scott Meredith Literary Agency, Inc.

"The Cat from Thebes" from *Tutankhamen and Other Essays,* by Arthur Weigall, published by Thornton Butterworth, Ltd., 1923.

"The Cat That Walked by Himself" from *Just So Stories* by Rudyard Kipling, copyright © 1902 by Rudyard Kipling.

"A Fine Place for the Cat" from *The Casino and Other Stories* by Margaret Bonham; reprinted by permission of the author and her agents, Curtis Brown Ltd., London.

"Puss in Boots" by Charles Perrault; reprinted from the Old English version of the eighteenth century.

"The Castle of Carabas" from *The Cat's Cradle Book* by Sylvia Townsend Warner. Copyright © 1940 by Sylvia Townsend Warner; reprinted by permission of The Viking Press, Inc.

"The King of the Cats" by Stephen Vincent Benét from *The Selected Works of Stephen Vincent Benét,* published by Holt, Rinehart & Winston, Inc. Copyright © 1938 by Stephen Vincent Benét; copyright renewed © 1963 by Thomas C. Benét, Stephanie B. Mahin, and Rachel Benét Lewis; reprinted by permission of Brandt & Brandt.

"Space-Time for Springers" by Fritz Leiber. Copyright © 1958 by Ballantine Books, Inc.; reprinted by permission of the author and his agent, Robert P. Mills.

"The Chelsea Cat" by C. H. B. Kitchin from *A Book of Modern Ghosts,* edited by Lady Cynthia Asquith. Copyright © 1952, 1953 by Charles Scribner's Sons; reprinted by permission of the author's agents, David Higham Associates, Ltd.

"The Spy" by Mario Brand, copyright © 1964 by Conde Nast Publications, Inc. Originally published in *Analog Science Fiction* magazine. Reprinted by permission of the author.

Text illustrations from *Dessins sans Paroles des Chats* by Steinlen by Courtesy of The Cooper-Hewitt Museum of Design, Smithsonian Institution; illustrations for jacket and for text page 196 from *Chats et Autres Bêtes* by Georges Lecomte, illustrated by Steinlen.

F. R. Noble School Library
Eastern Conn. State College
Willimantic, Conn. 06226

For Bob Lowndes, who provided Antigone, our First Cat.
For Bob Feldstein, who produced the next three.
And for my Bob, who took them all in.

Contents

ix

Kitten Caboodle

Introduction

by ROBERT SILVERBERG

I hope I don't sound too prejudiced when I say that the editor of this collection of stories about cats is ideally qualified to compile such a book. She has been married to a professional writer (me) for a good many years, and for all but three months of that time she has also shared her household with cats—sometimes twenty at a time. Obviously her firsthand experience with the problems and challenges of a writer's life makes her an expert on literature. Even more obviously, her firsthand experience of the feline world makes her an expert on cats. It follows perfectly logically that such a woman must be an authority on the literature of cats—and so she is. In this book she shares some of her favorite cat stories with you.

When we got married we had no particular intention to get involved with cats. We both liked cats, yes, and admired various animals who lived with various friends of ours. But neither of us had ever had a pet before, other than the usual frogs, turtles, and garter snakes that most children acquire and soon have to bury. (I had had a white mouse once, when I was about seven, a very neat and elegant animal, but it stayed in our house only until my mother found out about it. And then there was the eel I kept in the bathtub, briefly—she found that too.)

About three months after our marriage we spent a weekend at the country home of some friends. They had always had cats, and just then they also had kittens of an age well past the giving-away stage. The kittens were about half-grown, in fact, and from the moment we arrived on Friday afternoon we were subjected to a good deal of talk about taking one home. I scoffed. A soft white cat with some miscellaneous blotches on her sides was thrust at me. I had to admit that she was a sleek, affectionate, and intelligent animal, and beautiful, besides. I think her most impressive feature was a full, graceful dark tail tipped with a magnificent tuft of white fur. Barbara suggested that we take her home, and somehow I found myself accepting, and when we left that house on Sunday night we had a most unexpected package with us.

It must begin that way with nearly everyone. We named her Antigone, showed her around our still largely unfurnished Manhattan apartment, stocked up on catfood, catnip, sand basins, and other accessories, and began to read books on How To Raise Cats. Almost immediately we had a surgical crisis: one December evening Antigone decided to munch on a colorful bit of thread and swallowed it all—including the sewing needle at one end. I saw the glint of the needle as she swallowed it, and off we went in search of a cat hospital. For a week we were catless while our new pet was being repaired, and we discovered then just how important she had become in the household. In time she returned, quite healthy and very puzzled about the patch of missing fur on her side where she had undergone her operation. The fur grew back, but we were more careful about sewing needles thereafter.

Three years passed. Antigone grew wise and lovely. She was more my cat than Barbara's, since as a writer working at home I could spend twenty-four hours a day with her, while my wife was more like an occasional visitor. During the day Antigone watched me write and sometimes offered her opinions. At night she amused herself with acrobatics—I have never known a more agile cat, and Antigone was usually to be found grinning down like a Cheshire cat from the top of some lofty bookcase or door—and her last chore before bedtime was to march around counting the rooms of our apartment to make sure they were all there. We had five and a half rooms then, and that was as high as she could count.

It began to seem as if Antigone might be lonely. I resisted the idea of getting a second cat, but Barbara prevailed. A different set of friends produced a wobbly eight-week-old thing which, I was told, was a male Siamese kitten. I was unimpressed by his pedigree. We named him Radames, but for a while, watching him scuttle around the apartment, we called him Cockroach. I was not fond of him. I resented his intrusion into the house, and allowed him to stay only because Antigone had given him a friendly greeting the evening he arrived. Soon after, he chewed four pages out of a book I had been reading (I left the book open while answering a telephone call, and came back to find confetti all over the floor) and I liked him even less. But as he grew bigger he grew less wild, and he turned out to be handsome (if you overlooked his crossed eyes), affectionate, and cheerful. I no longer minded having two cats.

One problem developed. We had obtained Radames as a mate for Antigone. But Antigone, as she aged, turned into something of a grumpy old maid. She growled and hissed when Radames came near her. Since he was now full grown and quite masculine, he found this situation depressing, and so did we. I had to admit that we needed a *third* cat—to keep Radames company.

By this time we had moved from our apartment to a huge old house that could accommodate any quantity of cats, so there were no problems of adjustment. We acquired a female Siamese kitten, Radames' half-sister. Since our first two cats had such fancy names, I chose to name the newcomer Fred, though Barbara still insists sometimes that she should be called Aida.

Fred is not a very interesting cat, I'm afraid. She's soft and cuddly and a little slow-witted, and her only distinguishing feature is the remarkable right-angle bend in her tail. But Radames likes her very much, and she is an excellent mother who through the years has had dozens of kittens. Now we had three cats, and that seemed quite enough—especially since Fred and Antigone sometimes feuded and went roaring through the house, scattering manuscripts and knocking over flowerpots. One spring day Radames went off for a walk, though, and when after three dismal weeks he did not return we concluded we had better get ourselves a new tom— as a companion for Fred. Another obliging set of friends sent us a whole litter of Siamese kittens—two male, three female —and told us to take our pick and give away the rest. We chose a handsome little tom, and named him Ptolemy. Somehow we also kept (mainly because she hid under a radiator and refused to be evicted till we promised that she could stay) a mean, snarly, extremely beautiful female who had to be called Jezebel. Then Radames came home, hungry but healthy. He told us that he had investigated the neighborhood long enough, and was ready to settle down with us again. So of course Ptolemy had to go—no one in his right mind keeps two tomcats under one roof. But Jezebel remained.

And so we came to have four cats, although few of our

guests realized that, since Jezebel turned out to be quite shy and fled into hiding at the sound of a doorbell. Radames was quite happy with his little harem, and hordes of kittens arrived here, spent two months growing up, and were thrust off on friends. Antigone did not seem pleased by this invasion of the Siamese army, but she spent most of her time on the top floor of the house, helping me write, and did not have to see her rivals too often.

Poor old Antigone died one winter while we were on vacation. She had been in good health when we went away, and since she was only eight years old, her death was somewhat mysterious. I felt her loss deeply, because she was the only one of our four cats willing to be a typewriter cat. Radames, Fred, and Jezebel simply refused to sit around all day watching me work. So for five months I got along without a working cat, and didn't enjoy it; but I made no effort to find a replacement. One June afternoon a neighbor appeared, holding a calico cat. "Is this one of yours?" she asked. She wasn't. She was evidently a stray pet, but not one of our stray pets. We took her in, advertised for her owners, got no replies, and kept her. We gave her the fine old Anglo-Saxon name of Griddlebone. Griddlebone is an ideal cat for a working writer; she lacks Antigone's ability to soar through the air, but she is otherwise a perfect replacement, and she has lovely kittens, besides—black, orange, and white in varying mixtures. Since all of our other cats are Siamese and thus look more or less alike, Griddlebone and her multicolored broods add a touch of gaiety to the house.

Four cats, then. The kittens come and go—I suppose there have been two hundred of them over the years. If rearing that many cats and seeing them through all the troubles feline flesh is heir to does not qualify Barbara as an expert on the species *Felis*, I can't imagine what would. She also reads all that I write and is unsparing in her comments thereon, so I *know* she's an authority on the written word. She has combined those two special skills to produce this volume of cat lore, and I trust you won't think I'm showing prejudice when I say that she's done a pretty good job.

A P. S. by the editor:

I must, first of all, thank my resident writer for the glowing introduction he has provided for this anthology. It was quite generous of him to allow me to intrude upon his hallowed domain of literature at all—and to crown my endeavors in this domain with his delightful contribution was beyond the call of duty, and much appreciated. Unfortunately, he was so carried away with his talk of our feline family that he forgot to say anything about the book he was introducing. And so I take this opportunity to add a postscript, just to give you a hint of what is to follow.

The selections in this anthology span more than six centuries of literary history, and run the gamut from fairy tales to science fiction; they include ghost stories, horror tales, serious and not-so-serious poems, fantasies, and romances. But they all have one thing in common: cats—quite special cats, uniquely talented cats, unusually perceptive cats. This should not surprise us in the least, for who would take the trouble to tell the tale of an ordinary, run-of-the-mill cat? Or is it that there really is no such creature as an "ordinary cat" at all?

Certainly Smith is no run-of-the-mill cat—but then Smith is a writer, and writers, of course, are all quite special, whether cats or not. And there's Fritz Leiber's Gummitch, with his engrossing explanation of why there's another Gummitch on the other side of every mirror, while on the other side of every window, made of exactly the same material, there's inevitably a squirrel.

Another "thinking cat" is Phut Phat, who plays detective in a charming cat-mystery by Lilian Jackson Braun. People prove unequal to Phut Phat's perceptive powers, but he finally gets his point across. We also make the acquaintance of Théophile Gautier's logical Madame Théophile, whose feline reasoning leads her very far astray—for the caged parrot turns out not to be a green chicken at all.

Some old favorites appear here too: Charles Perrault's classic tale "Puss in Boots," Rudyard Kipling's Just So Story of "The Cat That Walked by Himself," and the age-old legend of Dick Whittington's cat, which we have read or been told many times before, and will never tire of hearing again.

Stephen Vincent Benét, in his strange version of the old tale of "The King of the Cats," introduces us to Princess Vivrakanarda, with fathomless blue eyes and a voice like golden velvet, and to Monsieur Tibault, who conducts an orchestra with his tail. Another story with its roots in the tangle of old legends is Sylvia Townsend Warner's "The Castle of Carabas," a tale full of carved wooden cats, plaster cats, stone cats, and cat's paw birthmarks, of superstitions and haunted houses—a tale of the hereditary hatred of the CAT. Also in the realm of witchcraft is C. H. B. Kitchin's story of a porcelain cat which brings upon its series of owners a succession of strange fates. The Chelsea Cat, in its china-cabinet, looks far too innocent to have been the cause of so many catastrophes.

In a world of its own is P. G. Wodehouse's hilarious story of Webster, a cat who ruled a roost in which he was an uninvited guest, and was well on the way to taking over the world when. . . . No, I'll let you discover the cause of Webster's downfall on your own, for the time has come to turn you loose in *Kitten Caboodle*. I hope you find as much pleasure in wandering through this basket of cat tales as I found in filling it.

June, 1968   Barbara Silverberg

1.

Phut Phat Concentrates

by LILIAN JACKSON BRAUN

Lilian Jackson Braun is well-known to fans of the mystery story; among her many tales are several cat-mysteries, of which "Phut Phat Concentrates" is my favorite. Miss Braun's cats inevitably regard themselves (and frequently prove themselves) to be brighter and more perceptive than people. Phut Phat goes far to demonstrate this point—despite certain difficulties in communication—finally drawing the encouraging conclusion that there may yet be some small hope for the human race.

PHUT PHAT knew, at an early age, that humans were an inferior breed. They were unable to see in the dark. They ate and drank unthinkable concoctions. And they had only five senses; the two who lived with Phut Phat could not even transmit their thoughts without resorting to words.

For more than a year, ever since he had arrived at the town house, Phut Phat had been attempting to introduce his system of communication, but his two pupils had made scant progress.

At dinner time he would sit in a corner, concentrating, and suddenly they would say, "Time to feed the cat," as if it were their own idea.

Their ability to grasp Phut Phat's messages extended only to the bare necessities of daily living, however. Beyond that, nothing ever got through to them, and it seemed unlikely that they would ever increase their powers.

Nevertheless, life in the town house was comfortable enough. It followed a fairly dependable routine, and to Phut Phat, routine was the greatest of all goals. He deplored such deviations as tardy meals, loud noises, unexplained persons on the premises, or liver during the week. He always had liver on Sunday.

It was a fashionable part of the city in which Phut Phat lived. His home was a three-story brick house furnished with thick rugs and down-cushioned chairs and tall pieces of furniture from which he could look down on questionable visitors. He could rise to the top of a highboy in a single leap, and when he chose to scamper from first-floor kitchen to second-floor living room to third-floor bedroom, his ascent up the carpeted staircase was very close to flight, for Phut Phat was a Siamese. His fawn-colored coat was finer than ermine. His eight seal-brown points (there had been nine before that trip to the hospital) were as sleek as panne velvet, and his slanted eyes brimmed with a mysterious blue.

Those who lived with Phut Phat in the town house were a pair, identified in his consciousness as ONE and TWO. It was ONE who supplied the creature comforts—beef on weekdays, liver on Sunday, and a warm cuddle now and then. She also fed his vanity with lavish compliments and adorned his throat with jeweled collars taken from her own wrists.

TWO, on the other hand, was valued chiefly for games and entertainment. He said very little, but he jingled keys at the end of a shiny chain and swung them back and forth for Phut Phat's amusement. And every morning in the dressing room he swished a necktie in tantalizing arcs while Phut Phat leaped and grabbed with pearly claws.

These daily romps, naps on downy cushions, outings in the coop on the fire escape, and two meals a day constituted the pattern of Phut Phat's life.

Then one Sunday he sensed a disturbing lapse in the household routine. The Sunday papers, usually scattered all over the library floor for him to shred with his claws, were stacked neatly on the desk. Furniture was rearranged. The house was filled with flowers, which he was not allowed to chew. All day long ONE was nervous, and TWO was too busy to play. A stranger in a white coat arrived and clattered glassware, and when Phut Phat went to investigate an aroma of shrimp and smoked oysters in the kitchen, the maid shooed him away.

Phut Phat seemed to be in everyone's way. Finally he was deposited in his wire coop on the fire escape, where he watched sparrows in the garden below until his stomach felt empty. Then he howled to come indoors.

He found ONE at her dressing table, fussing with her hair and unmindful of his hunger. Hopping lightly to the table, he sat erect among the sparkling bottles, stiffened his tail, and fastened his blue eyes on ONE's forehead. In that attitude he concentrated—and concentrated—and concentrated. It was never easy to communicate with ONE. Her mind hopped about like a sparrow, never relaxed, and Phut Phat had to strain every nerve to convey his meaning.

Suddenly ONE darted a look in his direction. A thought had occurred to her.

"Oh, John," she called to TWO, who was brushing his hair in the dressing room, "would you ask Millie to feed Phuffy? I forgot his dinner until this very minute. It's after five o'clock, and I haven't fixed my hair yet. You'd better put your coat on; people will start coming soon. And please tell Howard to light the candles. You might stack some records on the stereo, too . . . No, wait a minute. If Millie is still working on the canapes, would you feed Phuffy yourself? Just give him a slice of cold roast."

At this, Phut Phat stared at ONE with an intensity that made his thought waves almost visible.

"Oh, John, I forgot," she corrected. "It's Sunday, and he should have liver. Cut it in long strips or he'll toss it up. And before you do that, will you zip the back of my dress and put my emerald bracelet on Phuffy? Or maybe I'll wear the emerald myself, and he can have the topaz . . . John! Do you realize it's five fifteen? I wish you'd put your coat on."

"And I wish you'd simmer down," said TWO. "No one ever comes on time. Why do you insist on giving big parties, Helen, if it makes you so nervous?"

"Nervous? I'm not nervous. Besides, it was *your* idea to invite my friends and your clients at the same time. You said we should kill a whole blasted flock of birds with one stone . . . Now, *please*, John, are you going to feed Phuffy? He's staring at me and making my head ache."

Phut Phat scarcely had time to swallow his meal, wash his face, and arrange himself on the living room mantel before people started to arrive. His irritation at having the routine disrupted had been lessened somewhat by the prospect of be-

ing admired by the guests. His name meant "beautiful" in Siamese, and he was well aware of his pulchritude. Lounging between a pair of Georgian candlesticks, with one foreleg extended and the other exquisitely bent under at the ankle, with his head erect and gaze withdrawn, with his tail drooping nonchalantly over the edge of the marble mantel, he awaited compliments.

It was a large party, and Phut Phat observed that very few of the guests knew how to pay their respects to a cat. Some talked nonsense in a falsetto voice. Others made startling movements in his direction or, worse still, tried to pick him up.

There was one knowledgeable guest, however, who approached the mantel with a proper attitude of deference and reserve. Phut Phat squeezed his eyes in appreciation. The admirer was a man, who leaned heavily on a shiny stick. Standing at a respectful distance, he slowly held out his hand with one finger extended, and Phut Phat twitched his whiskers in polite acknowledgment.

"You are a living sculpture," said the man.

"That's Phut Phat," said ONE, who had pushed through the crowded room toward the fireplace. "He's the head of our household."

"He is obviously a champion," said the man with the shiny cane, addressing his hostess in the same dignified manner that had charmed Phut Phat.

"Yes, he could probably win a few ribbons if we wanted to enter him in shows, but he's strictly a pet. He never goes out, except in his coop on the fire escape."

"A coop? That's a splendid idea," said the man. "I should like to have one for my own cat. She's a tortoise-shell long-hair. May I inspect this coop before I leave?"

"Of course. It's just outside the library window."

"You have a most attractive house."

"Thank you. We've been accused of decorating it to complement Phut Phat's coloring, which is somewhat true. You'll notice we have no breakable bric-a-brac. When a Siamese flies through the air, he recognizes no obstacles."

"Indeed, I have noticed you collect Georgian silver," the man said in his courtly way. "You have some fine examples."

"Apparently you know silver. Your cane is a rare piece."

"Yes, it is an attempt to extract a little pleasure from a sorry necessity." He hobbled a step or two.

"Would you like to see my silver collection downstairs in the dining room?" asked ONE. "It's all early silver—about the time of Wren."

At this point Phut Phat, aware that the conversation no longer centered on him, jumped down from the mantel and stalked out of the room with several irritable flicks of the tail. He found an olive and pushed it down the heat register. Several feet stepped on him. In desperation he went upstairs to the guest room, where he discovered a mound of sable and mink and went to sleep.

After this upset in the household routine Phut Phat needed several days to catch up on his rest—so the ensuing week was a sleepy blur. But soon it was Sunday again, with liver for breakfast, Sunday papers scattered over the floor, and everyone sitting around being pleasantly routine.

"Phuffy! Don't roll on those newspapers," said ONE. "John, can't you see the ink rubs off on his fur? Give him the *Wall Street Journal*—it's cleaner."

"Maybe he'd like to go outside in his coop and get some sun."

"That reminds me, dear. Who was that charming man with

the silver cane at our party? I didn't seem to catch his name."

"I don't know," said TWO. "I thought he was someone you invited."

"Well, he wasn't. He must have come with one of the other guests. At any rate, he was interested in getting a coop like ours for his own cat. He has a long-haired torty. And did I tell you the Hendersons have two Burmese kittens? They want us to go over and see them next Sunday and have a drink."

Another week passed, during which Phut Phat discovered a new perch. He found he could jump to the top of an antique armoire—a towering piece of furniture in the hall outside the library. Otherwise, it was a routine week, followed by a routine week-end, and Phut Phat was content.

ONE and TWO were going out on Sunday evening to see the Burmese kittens, so Phut Phat was served an early dinner and soon afterward he fell asleep on the library sofa.

When the telephone rang and waked him, it was dark and he was alone. He raised his head and chattered at the instrument until it stopped its noise. Then he went back to sleep, chin on paw.

The second time the telephone started ringing, Phut Phat stood up and scolded it, arching his body in a vertical stretch and making a question mark with his tail. To express his annoyance, he hopped on the desk and sharpened his claws on *Webster's Unabridged*. Then he spent quite some time chewing on a leather bookmark. After that he felt thirsty. He sauntered toward the powder room for a drink.

No lights were burning, and no moonlight came through the windows, yet he moved through the dark rooms with assurance, side-stepping table legs and stopping to examine infinitesimal particles on the hall carpet. Nothing escaped him.

Phut Phat was lapping water, and the tip of his tail was waving rapturously from side to side, when something caused him to raise his head and listen. His tail froze. Sparrows in the backyard? Rain on the fire escape? There was silence again. He lowered his head and resumed his drinking.

A second time he was alerted. Something was happening that was not routine. His tail bushed like a squirrel's, and with his whiskers full of alarm he stepped noiselessly into the hall, peering toward the library.

Someone was on the fire escape. Something was gnawing at the library window.

Petrified, he watched—until the window opened and a dark figure slipped into the room. With one lightning glide Phut Phat sprang to the top of the tall armoire.

There on his high perch, able to look down on the scene, he felt safe. But was it enough to feel safe? His ancestors had been watch-cats in Oriental temples centuries before. They had hidden in the shadows and crouched on high walls, ready to spring on any intruder and tear his face to ribbons —just as Phut Phat shredded the Sunday paper. A primitive instinct rose in his breast, but quickly it was quelled by civilized inhibitions.

The figure in the window advanced stealthily toward the hall, and Phut Phat experienced a sense of the familiar. It was the man with the shiny stick. This time, though, his presence smelled sinister. A small blue light now glowed from the head of the cane, and instead of leaning on it, the man pointed it ahead to guide his way out of the library and to-ward the staircase. As the intruder passed the armoire, Phut Phat's fur rose to form a sharp ridge down his spine. Instinct said, "Spring at him!" But vague fears held him back.

With feline stealth the man moved downstairs, unaware of

two glowing diamonds that watched him in the blackness, and Phut Phat soon heard noises in the dining room. He sensed evil. Safe on top of the armoire, he trembled.

When the man reappeared, he was carrying a bulky load, which he took to the library window. Then he crept to the third floor, and there were muffled sounds in the bedroom. Phut Phat licked his nose in apprehension.

Now the man reappeared, following a pool of blue light. As he approached the armoire, Phut Phat shifted his feet, bracing himself against something invisible. He felt a powerful compulsion to attack, and yet a fearful dismay.

"Get him!" commanded a savage impulse within him.
"Stay!" warned the fright throbbing in his head.
"Get him! ... Now ... now ... NOW!"

Phut Phat sprang at the man's head, ripping with razor claws wherever they sank into flesh.

The hideous scream that came from the intruder was like an electric shock; it sent Phut Phat sailing through space—up the stairs—into the bedroom—under the bed.

For a long time he quaked uncontrollably, his mouth parched and his ears inside out with horror at what had happened. There was something strange and wrong about it, although its meaning eluded him. Waiting for Time to heal his confusion, he huddled there in darkness and privacy. Blood soiled his claws. He sniffed with distaste and finally was compelled to lick them clean. He did it slowly and with repugnance. Then he tucked his paws under his warm body and waited.

When ONE and TWO came home, he sensed their arrival even before the taxicab door slammed. He should have bounded to meet them, but the experience had left him in a daze, quivering internally, weak and unsure. He heard the rattle of the front door lock, feet climbing the stairs, and the click of the light switch in the room where he waited in bewilderment under the bed.

ONE instantly gave a gasp, then a shriek. "John! Someone's been in this room. We've been robbed!"

TWO's voice was incredulous. "What! How do you know?"

"My jewel case. Look! It's open—and empty!"

TWO threw open a closet door. "Your furs are still here, Helen. What about money? Did you have any money in the house?"

"I never leave money around. But the silver! What about the silver? John, go down and see. I'm afraid to look . . . No! Wait a minute!" ONE's voice rose in panic. "Where's Phut Phat? What's happened to Phut Phat?"

"I don't know," said TWO with alarm. "I haven't seen him since we came in."

They searched the house, calling his name—unaware, with their limited senses, that Phut Phat was right there under the bed, brooding over the upheaval in his small world, and now and then licking his claws.

When at last, crawling on their hands and knees, they spied two eyes glowing red under the bed, they drew him out gently. ONE hugged him with a rocking embrace and rubbed her face, wet and salty, on his fur, while TWO stood by, stroking him with a heavy hand. Comforted and reassured, Phut Phat stopped trembling. He tried to purr, but the shock had constricted his larynx.

ONE continued to hold Phut Phat in her arms—and he had no will to jump down—even after two strange men were admitted to the house; they asked questions and examined all the rooms.

"Everything is insured," ONE told them, "but the silver is

irreplaceable. It's old and very rare. Is there any chance of getting it back, Lieutenant?" She fingered Phut Phat's ears nervously.

"At this point it's hard to say," the detective said. "But you may be able to help us. Have you noticed any strange incidents lately? Any unusual telephone calls?"

"Yes," said ONE. "Several times recently the phone has rung, and when we answered it, there was no one on the line."

"That's the usual method. They wait until they know you're not at home."

ONE gazed into Phut Phat's eyes. "Did the phone ring tonight while we were out, Phuffy?" she asked, shaking him lovingly. "If only Phut Phat could tell us what happened! He must have had a terrifying experience. Thank heaven he wasn't harmed."

Phut Phat raised his paw to lick between his toes, still defiled with human blood.

"If only Phuffy could tell us who was here!"

Phut Phat paused with toes spread and pink tongue extended. He stared at ONE's forehead

"Have you folks noticed any strangers in the neighborhood?" the lieutenant was asking. "Anyone who would arouse suspicion?"

Phut Phat's body tensed, and his blue eyes, brimming with knowledge, bored into that spot above ONE's eyebrows.

"No, I can't think of anyone," she said. "Can you, John?"

TWO shook his head.

"Poor Phuffy," said ONE. "See how he stares at me; he must be hungry. Does Phuffy want a little snack?"

Phut Phat squirmed.

"About those bloodstains on the window sill," said the detective. "Would the cat attack an intruder viciously enough to draw blood?"

"Heavens no!" said ONE. "He's just a pampered little house pet. We found him hiding under the bed, scared stiff."

"And you're sure you can't remember any unusual incident lately? Has anyone come to the house who might have seen the silver or jewelry? Repairman? Window washer?"

"I wish I could be more helpful," said ONE, "but honestly, I can't think of a single suspect."

Phut Phat gave up!

Wriggling free, he jumped down from ONE's lap and walked toward the door with head depressed and hind legs stiff with disgust. He knew who it was. He knew! The man with the shiny stick. But it was useless to try to communicate. The human mind was closed so tight that nothing important would ever penetrate. And ONE was so busy with her own chatter that her mind . . .

The jingle of keys caught Phut Phat's attention. He turned and saw TWO swinging his key chain back and forth, back and forth, and saying nothing. TWO always did more thinking than talking. Perhaps Phut Phat had been trying to communicate with the wrong mind. Perhaps TWO was really Number One in the household and ONE was Number Two.

Phut Phat froze in his position of concentration, sitting tall and compact with tail stiff. The key chain swung back and forth, and Phut Phat fastened his blue eyes on three wrinkles, just underneath TWO's hairline. He concentrated. The key chain swung back and forth, back and forth. Phut Phat kept concentrating.

"Wait a minute," said TWO, coming out of his puzzled silence. "I just thought of something. Helen, remember that party we gave a couple of weeks ago? There was one guest we couldn't account for. A man with a silver cane."

"Why, yes! The man was so curious about the coop on the fire escape. Why didn't I think of him? Lieutenant, he was terribly interested in our Georgian silver."

TWO said, "Does that suggest anything to you, Lieutenant?"

"Yes, it does." The detective exchanged nods with his partner.

"This man," ONE volunteered, "had a very cultivated voice and a charming manner."

"We know him," the detective said grimly. "We know his method. What you tell us fits perfectly. But we didn't know he was operating in this neighborhood again."

ONE said, "What mystifies me is the blood on the window sill."

Phut Phat arched his body in a long, luxurious stretch and walked from the room, looking for a soft, dark, quiet place. Now he would sleep. He felt relaxed and satisfied. He had made vital contact with a human mind, and perhaps—after all—there was hope. Some day they might learn the system, learn to open their minds and receive. They had a long way to go before they realized their potential—but there was hope.

F. R. Noble School Library
Eastern Conn. State College
Willimantic, Conn. 06226

2.

On the Death of a Favourite Cat, Drowned in a Tub of Gold-Fishes

by THOMAS GRAY

'Twas on a lofty vase's side,
Where China's gayest art had dyed
   The azure flowers that blow,
Demurest of the tabby kind,
The pensive Selima, reclined,
   Gazed on the lake below.

Her conscious tail her joy declared;
The air round face, the snowy beard,
   The velvet of her paws,
Her coat that with the tortoise vies,
Her ears of jet and emerald eyes,
   She saw, and purred applause.

Still had she gazed, but 'midst the tide
Two angel forms were seen to glide,—
   The Genii of the stream:
Their scaly armour's Tyrian hue,
Through richest purple, to the view
   Betrayed a golden gleam.

The hapless nymph with wonder saw:
A whisker first, and then a claw,
 With many an ardent wish,
She stretched in vain to reach the prize;
What female heart can gold despise?
 What cat's averse to fish?

Presumptuous maid! with looks intent,
Again she stretched, again she bent,
 Nor knew the gulf between.
Malignant Fate sat by and smiled,
The slippery verge her feet beguiled,
 She stumbled headlong in.

Eight times emerging from the flood,
She mewed to every watery god
 Some speedy aid to send.
No Dolphin came, no Nereid stirred,
Nor cruel Tom nor Susan heard;
 A favourite has no friend!

From hence, ye Beauties! undeceived,
Know one false step is ne'er retrieved,
 And be with caution bold:
Not all that tempts your wandering eyes
And heedless hearts is lawful prize,
 Nor all that glisters, gold.

3.

Smith

by ANN CHADWICK

I know nothing at all about Ann Chadwick other than the fact that she has written the most delightful, most terrifying cat story I have ever read. Through Miss Chadwick we make the acquaintance of Smith, tragic, talented Smith, who *was* a writer—who *is* a cat—and who is determined to make the best, a hilarious, bewildering best, of a very peculiar situation.

W<small>E</small> took a long time to waken. The voice seemed to be shouting in our dreams, until both achieving consciousness at about the same time, we heard it wailing in the street.

Our eyes sprang wide open on the darkness. M. said, It's a drunk. But the pub had been shut two hours when we went to bed. I murmured some answer without much confidence. M. tried to be reassuring. He's passed out somewhere, and now he's wakened and can't see.

Neither of us moved. The voice called regularly, loudly, on a slowly rising note of despair. Help! Help! Help! Why doesn't somebody help me?

It went on . . . we lay motionless. There was a considerable weight on my chest which seemed to prevent me stirring even to sigh. Slowly tapping steps bore it past; and as they began at last to fade it grew sharply higher, becoming a mad shout. Then, on a terrible note of panic, with spell-breaking suddenness, it stopped.

M. grunted at the shock. We rose out of bed in a single effortless surge and stumbled to the window, bumping into one another in our haste. The moon was down, but a hatful of stars shone palely into the dark street. There was no one there. Not even an echo of the awful voice remained, except for the moans of two tom cats in the gutter. Wondering why they had not been frightened off I peered at them. Something the size of a cushion lay in the road.

Look, I said. Where? said M. Beside that cat. I can't see anything. But there's something down there. Where? he said, I can't see anything . . . it's another cat. No it's not, I insisted, I'm going to see. M. made a spooky laugh. You can if you like; I'm going to bed.

I turned on every light in the house on the way down. I had said I was going to see. After some slight hesitation I opened the door and shone my torch out in the road. One of the cats turned and fled. The other looked at the light with eyes like new pennies. Beside it lay the shadow that had raised my curiosity. From where I stood it looked like a shabby black coat.

Then the cat came forward in a half run. In the light from the doorway I was it was a dirty, undersized ginger tom. Go on! I said, backing from the door and thinking to shut it in his face. I had underestimated him. He slipped between my

pyjama leg and the jamb and had reached the first stair before
the door slammed shut. Don't leave my clothes out there! he
said.

I reached for him. You come here, I said. Then I realized
that he had spoken. I straightened up slowly. In sudden emer-
gencies I have trained my mind to go blank so as to avoid
panic. I didn't panic. What's going on here? I said coldly. A
curtain of mauve gauze enveloped my mind.

When I found myself listening again the cat was saying: I
don't know. . . . I must be going crazy. His voice was familiar.

You're going crazy! I gasped incredulously but with some
measure of relief. Is it Smith? Yes, said Smith. You've left
my clothes out there. I shook my head vaguely. What in the
name of God happened to you?

Smith was a writer, who lived three streets away in
wretched digs over a garage. He was a writer of promise and
of some slight celebrity. His short stories were obscure and
his critical essays incomprehensible. His manners were appalling and his friends were very few.

I had never liked Smith, or been his friend. But now the
misery in his yellow, shifting eyes, and in the droop of his
soiled whiskers, touched me strangely.

Come on up and show M. what's happened, I said.

But my clothes! . . . My identity card!

Damn your clothes. You won't need them now. He followed me with a groan.

M., I said, look.

M. pulled the edge of the eiderdown from in front of his
eyes and looked at Smith. How did it get in? he demanded.

Well, I said, it's not actually a bona fide cat. M. looked at
me strangely. Put that stinking thing out, he said. It's two
o'clock.

Smith said, If you put me out now, that bloody tom cat will get me and it will be murder.

M. reached for his dressing gown and got out of bed and put it on. He sat down on the edge of the bed and looked slowly from me to Smith, and from Smith to me. Now, what on earth is happening? said M.

The surprising thing about the rest of the night, which we spent in a rising fever of conversation, was that Smith, who had begun in a state of bewildered despair, grew calmer and more rational as it wore on. His usual reaction to any interference with the serene course of his career (and there had been many an interference) was to grow quickly profane and ultimately hysterical. He was celebrated for spectacular scenes in cafes and in buses. But overtaken by real disaster and finding himself a survivor, after a fashion, he seemed prepared to accept the situation with good grace, even to find it a fittingly distinctive one. By morning he was almost flattered by it. As a situation after all it must have been unique.

His only apprehension was that M. or I might carelessly expose him to the attacks of other cats. I hate cats, he explained. I've always hated and envied them. They have no self-respect, you know. His yellow eyes flickered, and his pink tongue slipped for a moment over the short, faded whiskers. No worries. No ideals. No conscience. Cats are the only really free creatures on earth. They could be happy if they had the wit.

He glanced round in the old way, assuring himself of the attention of his audience. M. and I watched fascinated, however, and this eloquent cat had better listeners than the man.

. . . Their sensitivity brings them no unhappiness, but only greater pleasure. They are unashamed of cunning, of laziness, of any of their useful characteristics. They're hateful. His whiskers lay on his narrow, dirty cheeks tightly, almost sleekly, and his tongue protruded for a moment between his lips in satisfaction. I could not take my eyes from him. If he had been unpleasant as a man, as a cat he was loathsome.

But about his transformation he said very little; there was very little, he claimed, to tell. There had been no warning, no sensation to describe; he had simply been one minute a man and the next a cat. And what, I asked, had he been doing at that hour in the street calling for help?

It was a bet, said Smith. Jerry bet me I could walk all the way from the Embankment to King's Road shouting for help, but not a soul would stir to help me. He smirked at me then. But you came down, he said.

Only because you stopped, I said. Where was Jerry?

Smith frowned. He was right with me, to see I didn't cheat, and to keep an eye out for coppers. M. and I looked at him blankly for a moment. He looked blankly back. The other tom. Slowly our faces showed that we had come to the same conclusion. Poor cat, said Smith, I don't even remember what he looked like.

The next week brought a series of developments, and established the relations with Smith which we were to enjoy for some time after. His clothes had been picked up by the police early in the first day, together with Jerry's, and the two had been posted as missing. Not thirty-six hours later there was a sensational story in all the papers about a cat that had been picked up in Sloane Square asking people for threepence for a cup of coffee. He had been rushed to the research laboratories of a famous hospital and had undergone extensive experiments in the cause of science. Unfortunately, he had died of exhaustion and hunger before they could be completed. There was a great furore over it, and the scientists involved received a great deal of publicity for their abstruse theories on the phenomenon.

The excitement died down; but it left another fear in Smith's heart to live with his fear of other cats. The power of men of science, which until now he had been content to scorn as an artist, he now dreaded as a possible subject. I must admit that we were not unpleased to have these holds upon him; for we still saw him as the old Smith, difficult and unreliable.

Among our own three cats, cn the morning upon which Smith first entered the kitchen with me, discussing breakfast, there was the most appalling confusion and disorder. Frummitt, the Siamese, opened her blue eyes wide and would certainly have flown at him had not the kitten, rising up like a square ball of grey wool under the water heater, put his inflated tail into the lit gas-jet. He withdrew it smartly and rushed round the room closely followed by a stinking plume of black smoke, creating a lively diversion. The tabby stray, Pont, looked with sad resignation at the intruder, who looked like any cat but who laughed like a demon at the kitten's gyrations. Pont had always known in his heart that something unspeakably awful would happen to him some day. His melancholy features composed themselves in despair, and he scrambled into the vegetable bin.

I opened the last tin of decent sardines for Smith. This is ridiculous, I said. Cats don't get sardines around here; you'll just have to get used to scraps. Smith looked at me coldly. I hope you don't expect me to eat those out of the tin, he said. I shall buy my own food of course.

I laughed at him. At once I regretted it. O my God, said

Smith. His eyes travelled slowly from mine to his dirty paws. My typewriter. I was sorry for him again. You'll have to dictate, I said.

For the rest of the day Smith was inconsolable. I think it was only his dread of coming too much under my discipline that roused him to tackle the problem again. We brought him a saucer of beer just before closing time. Smith, I said when we had finished, have a cigarette. I watched him struggle with it for some time until he had learned how to pinion it with one claw without unsheathing the others. He held it stiffly, and his anxiety made his whiskers stand out like a seal's. Tomorrow Smith, I said, we're going to have a bath. He saw his position immediately. There was a bad moment while I found the cigarette, which had rolled under my chair, and Smith got the smoke out of his lungs. I suppose it made him desperate.

There were seven dead fleas in the rinse water next day, but Smith was too taken up with plans and schemes to see them there. Can you get me an agent? he asked when he was sitting in front of the fire, drying.

Now look, Smith, I said, if you could have found an agent as Smith it wouldn't have been very surprising. But what agent is going to take your sort of stuff these days from an unknown writer? And, what's more, I haven't time to write it out for you, and I don't know who has. Why don't you concentrate on being a cat? If you dry without licking yourself smooth you'll look a sight. Smith looked at his fur over his shoulder with raised eyebrows. Lick this stuff? Don't be an ass. Now listen to my idea.

I sat watching him dry with his coat tufted in every direction. Gradually I realized that he was putting a pretty amazing proposal to me—for Smith. But Smith, I objected per-

versely, what about your "art"? He smirked, licking his fore-
paw once or twice without noticing what he was doing, and
slipping it inadvertently behind his ear. Actually, it was mostly
false pride, he said.

He cleared his throat. As a cat I have no self-respect, you
see. No one knows me. As a matter of fact it seems quite fantastic to me now that I was so anxious to make a name. I can
see now that I'm not *quite* so good as I perhaps thought then.
Never mind: now things are rather clearer to me. Can you
get crayfish on the black market?

Smith, I ventured, not without a certain note of respect,
you are despicable. Don't be a prig, said Smith. You don't
stand to lose. You'll have to find me an agent right away, and
take a chance on writing the first job out for me. You can have
twenty per cent.

I am not, after all, blind to opportunity. When the mauve
curtain had lifted I said firmly, I will be secretary *and* agent;
and I can have half.

M. was quite surprised. I didn't know he had it in him he
said. Make him get to work right away. There's a place near
the office where I can get it typed out for him.

I made out a list of all the women's magazines and papers;
and Smith dictated the first story to me in three evenings. It
was accepted by the first editor who saw it; and my half of
the cheque was enough to run the house for a month.

For a while I thought that Smith must be cheating. The stuff
poured out of him like syrup, effortlessly, endlessly, horribly.
I took it all down, the men and women blue and grey-eyed,
tall, lean, athletic, the brave smiles, the silent tears, the problems of unprecedented difficulty and the solutions of unbelievable sweetness and simplicity. I took down agonizing
situations of misunderstood nobility, of proud quarrels and ten-

der reconciliations, of simple hearts and true, of something Smith called Lerve. We gotta give them Lerve Lerve Lerve he said. And we did. We gotta give them ROmance, he said. We gave them ROmance. He had a bent for it, a talent, several talents.

I spent half of each day taking Smith's dictation, and more and more of each evening in checking correspondence and sending away the latest stories or instalments of stories. Smith's cupboard of tinned fish and meat, condensed milk, cake and cheese grew like a reassuring barrier between him and his old life. He had fresh meat at fantastic prices from a butcher recommended by the friend of a friend, he had game and oysters in season. He had cream, ice-cream and eggs from a fashionable dairy in town. All this without a ration book. His money was possessed by devils. Even the part of it that was mine went very often far astray in worthy enough causes.

We grew to like Smith more and more. As time went on, and we were able at last to afford servants so that I could finish my work with him in the day, we found ourselves spending more of our evenings over drinks and cigarettes with him in his room. Shorn of his fears and inhibitions he was a marvellously entertaining conversationalist. He liked still to hear all the news of the town he never saw; and we would sit by the hour with him gossiping about friends. He contributed an endless assortment of odd and revealing opinions from his new angle of approach to life; and we did not tire of his quaint and dreadful philosophy.

Pont and Frummitt became his devoted attendants, which was fortunate for his appearance. Only the kitten was unable to forgive. We had to give the proud creature away in the end, because its speed of growth so alarmed poor Smith. On his advice we took the kitten into Battersea and gave it to a man with a high wire fence round his front garden; rather late at night it was, too late I remember for a formal presentation.

Smith worked hard and lived well, and took a modest pride in the quantities of fan mail we got addressed to Kitty Smith. He used to say we soothed the minds and dulled the senses of half the women in Britain; and I must confess I enjoyed the admiration and envy of my friends, who were flatteringly surprised at my development from housewife to author. Sometimes Smith would tilt his furry face to one side and ask me whether I ever aspired to writing better stuff. He knew it upset me when he talked like that, and he was full of fun.

M. considered the advent of Smith the biggest stroke of luck that had ever come our way. After he had left his job and thrown the biggest party Chelsea ever saw to celebrate the event, he designed a new room for Smith and had it decorated with considerable splendour. Because Smith's stories were syndicated all over the world by this time, and his income was improving steadily.

He had been with us two years when he came to me about a novel. There's one thing I'd like to do, you know, he said, jumping on to my knee one afternoon. He settled himself carefully and pricked my knees with his long, sharp claws. Don't, I said. Sorry, said Smith, careless of me. I've always thought I could write a best seller . . . I sometimes used to think about it for weeks when I was hungry, and wonder if it could be done under a nom de plume so that none of my contemporaries would know. But I never did, you know . . . Pride. He brushed the long golden hairs of his bosom lightly with his tongue.

Oh, Smith, I said, lazily stroking his shining back, you're despicable. He wrote his novel. It was a great love story, built on a plot he had read in *Chums* when he was a kid. There were Roundheads and Royalists in it, and, of course, tender hearts and true. The hero, I remember, was tall, lean and athletic. We sold it to one of the big publishing houses seven months from that afternoon when he proposed beginning it, and six months later we were reading the reviews. They were not good reviews, but they didn't hurt the sales. As the publishers promised, it gave you thrills and chills and suspense, it left you with a smile on your lip and tears in your throat. It made five editions that year.

It was after the supper we had given to some Hollywood people who wanted to discuss film rights, that I visited Smith in his room and saw the first slight evidences of the change that was to overtake him. When I joined him after that supper he had himself just finished a tureen of clam chowder and was licking the last traces of cream carefully from his whiskers. Watching him, I tried to remember what the old ginger Smith had looked like. It was difficult; this corpulent and shining golden creature was a different cat.

The eyes that had glittered like pennies in the dark of that first awful night, now shone like pale moons from his round face. The once short and faded whiskers were like long white celluloid antennae, each sprouting stiffly from an ochre dot on his full and curling golden lip. His ochre ears with their pale buff linings of down, stood always half inclined at a polite and fastidious angle. His magnificent shoulders, and his bosom with its mayor's chain of an orange strip were sleek and full. The red fur of his flanks (which Frummitt was even now arranging with her careful tongue) lay above the swinging furry expanse of his paunch like the flanks of a tiger. And his long, thick tail, which swung with the languid power of a hemp hawser, brushed the carpet softly as he turned towards me. Ah, said Smith in welcome.

We chose a convenient level on the upholstered window-seat which ranged the glass-brick walls from floor to ceiling around Smith's room, and made ourselves comfortable. Smith lit a cigarette from the constant flame kept burning on one of the tables at various levels convenient to the seat. Then I saw him frown for the first time in many weeks. He turned from the cigarette and smiled at me wistfully. I think you know, he said, that my tastes are becoming more simple. I watched the cigarette burn itself out in the tray while we talked, and without realizing it watched the change in Smith begin.

The film rights for the novel brought us a great deal of money. We moved to our present home in the country, and there would have been a suite here for Smith, had he not preferred to have his old room reconstructed with a few simple omissions. He began to take great interest in having the real countryside to walk and wander in, and with Pont for his jealous and faithful guide even extended his evening exercise to a rabbit-riddled hillside of briers above the house. He gave up many of his more sophisticated pleasures; I do not remember his enjoying a drink with us since coming here. His movie projector in which he took such great delight only a few months ago has not even been used to show the film of his movie.

The climax came two weeks ago. It had been months since Smith and I had done any new work, and I was thinking about this one day as we sat in the sun watching the birds. I could feel his long claws prick my knees every time a tit swooped near for the crumbs from our tea. Don't, I said. Sorry, said Smith. Then I asked him about the work.

He didn't answer me. Instead he asked me another question. Would you have any objection to my marrying Frummitt? he said.

Good God! I exclaimed, no of course not. I was silent for a moment, thinking over all the changes we had noticed in Smith recently, and wondering to myself. Smith went on easily, She proposed to me this morning, he said. I really think it's not much to ask after all these years of devotion. And now, he added, with his usual gentle dignity, if it is all right with you I think I'll go in and tell her.

He got down from my lap and moved up the walk to the house with long silent steps like a mountain lion. His broad shoulders and slight back glinted in the sun, a brilliant red gold. On an impulse I almost called out to him; he seemed to be leaving us so irrevocably. M. had looked up from the frame where his young cucumbers were sleeping hotly. He watched Smith go up the walk and then turned to me and smiled. I smiled back at him, bewildered.

4.

The Retired Cat

by WILLIAM COWPER

A poet's cat, sedate and grave
As poet well could wish to have,
Was much addicted to inquire
For nooks to which she might retire,
And where, secure as mouse in chink,
She might repose, or sit and think.
I know not where she caught the trick,—
Nature perhaps herself had cast her
In such a mould *philosophique*,
Or else she learn'd it of her Master.
Sometimes ascending, debonair,
An apple-tree, or lofty pear,
Lodged with convenience in the fork,
She watched the gardener at his work;
Sometimes her ease and solace sought
In an old empty watering-pot;
There wanting nothing save a fan,
To seem some nymph in her sedan,
Apparell'd in exactest sort,
And ready to be borne to Court.
  But love of change it seems has place,
Not only in our wiser race;
Cats also feel, as well as we,
That passion's force, and so did she.

Her climbing she began to find
Exposed her too much to the wind,
And the old utensil of tin
Was cold and comfortless within;
She therefore wish'd, instead of those,
Some place of more serene repose,
Where neither cold might come, nor air
Too rudely wanton with her hair;
And sought it in the likeliest mode
Within her Master's snug abode.

   A drawer, it chanced, at bottom lined
With linen of the softest kind.
With such as merchants introduce
From India, for the ladies' use,
A drawer impending o'er the rest,
Half open in the topmost chest,
Of depth enough, and none to spare,
Invited her to slumber there;
Puss with delight beyond expression
Surveyed the scene and took possession.
Recumbent at her ease ere long,
And lull'd by her own humdrum song,
She left the cares of life behind,
And slept as she would sleep her last,
When in came, housewifely inclined,
The chambermaid, and shut it fast,
By no malignity impell'd,
But all unconscious whom it held.

   Awaken'd by the shock, cried Puss,
"Was ever cat attended thus!
The open drawer was left, I see,
Merely to prove a nest for me;

For soon as I was well composed,
Then came the maid, and it was closed.
How smooth these kerchiefs and how sweet,
Oh, what a delicate retreat!
I will resign myself to rest,
Till Sol, declining in the west,
Shall call to supper, when, no doubt,
Susan will come and let me out."
    The evening came, the sun descended,
And Puss remain'd still unattended.
The night rolled tardily away
(With her indeed 'twas never day),
The sprightly morn her course renew'd,
The evening grey again ensued,
And Puss came into mind no more
Than if entomb'd the day before.
With hunger pinch'd, and pinch'd for room,
She now presaged approaching doom,
Nor slept a single wink, nor purr'd,
Conscious of jeopardy incurr'd.
    That night by chance, the poet watching,
Heard an inexplicable scratching;
His noble heart went pit-a-pat,
And to himself he said,—"What's that?"
He drew the curtain at his side,
And forth he peep'd, but nothing spied;
Yet, by his ear directed, guess'd
Something imprisoned in the chest,
And, doubtful what, with prudent care
Resolved it should continue there.
At length, a voice which well he knew,
A long and melancholy mew,

Saluting his poetic ears,
Consoled him, and dispelled his fears.
He left his bed, he trod the floor,
He 'gan in haste the drawers explore,
The lowest first, and, without stop,
The rest in order to the top;
For 'tis a truth well known to most,
That whatsoever thing is lost,
We seek it, ere it come to light,
In every cranny but the right.
Forth skipp'd the cat, not now replete
As erst with airy self-conceit,
Nor in her own fond apprehension
A theme for all the world's attention;
But modest, sober, cured of all
Her notions hyperbolical,
And wishing for a place of rest
Anything rather than a chest.
Then stepp'd the poet into bed,
With this reflection in his head.

Moral.
Beware of too sublime a sense
Of your own worth and consequence.
The man who dreams himself so great,
And his importance of such weight,
That all around, in all that's done,
Must move and act for him alone,
Will learn in school of tribulation
The folly of his expectation.

5.

Dick Whittington

ANON.

Richard Whittington was an English merchant of the late fourteenth and early fifteenth centuries. When quite young, he ran away from home and, in the course of his adventures on the way to London, acquired a cat whose legend has become an accepted part of English folklore. (Similar legends exist also in German, Danish, Italian, and Russian tradition.) Through the good offices of his cat, Mr. Whittington established a large estate, contracted a suitable marriage, and became a great success in local politics, being "thrice Lord Mayor of London."

One Richard Whittington, supposed to have been an outcast, for he did not know his parents, they either dying or leaving him to the parish of Taunton Dean, in Somersetshire; but as he grew up, being displeased with the cruel usage of the nurse, he ran away from her at seven years of age and traveled about the country, living upon the charity of well-disposed persons, till he grew up to be a fine, sturdy youth; when at last, being threatened to be whipped if he continued in that idle course of life, he resolved to go to London, having heard that the streets were paved with gold. Not knowing the way, he followed the carriers, and at night, for the little service he did them in rubbing the horses, they gave him a supper. When he arrived in this famous city, the carriers, supposing he would be a troublesome hanger-on, told him plainly he must leave the inn and immediately seek out some employment, and gave him a groat. With this he wandered about, but, not knowing anyone, and being in tattered garb, some pitied him as a forlorn wretch, but few gave him anything.

What he had got being soon spent, his stomach craved supply; but not having anything to satisfy it, he resolved rather to starve than steal. After two hungry days, and lying on the hulks at night, weary and faint, he got to a merchant's house in Leadenhall Street, where he made many signs of his distressed condition; but the ill-natured cook was going to kick him from the door, saying, "If you tarry here, I will kick you into the kennel." This put him almost into despair, so he laid him down on the ground, being unable to go any farther. In the meantime, Mr. Fitz-Warren, whose house it was, came from the Royal Exchange, and seeing him there in that condition, demanded what he wanted and sharply told him if he did not immediately depart he would cause him to be sent to the House of Correction, calling him a lazy, idle fellow. On this he got up, and, after falling two or three times through faintness for want of food, and making a bow, told him he was a poor country fellow in a starving condition, and if that he might be put in a way, he would refuse no labor, if it was only for his victuals. This raised a Christian compassion in the merchant toward him, and then, wanting a scullion, he immediately ordered one of his servants to take him in, and gave orders how he should be employed; and so he was feasted to his great refreshment.

This was the first step of Providence to raise him to what in time made him to be the City's glory and the nation's wonder. But he met with many difficulties, for the servants made sport of him, and the ill-natured cook told him, "You are to come under me, so look sharp; clean the spit and the dripping-pan, make the fires, wind up the jack, and nimbly do all other scullery work that I may set you about, or else I will break your head with my ladle, and kick you about like a football."

This was cold comfort, but better than starving; and what gave him a gleam of hope was Mrs. Alice, his master's daughter, who hearing her father had entertained a new servant, came to see him, and ordered that he should be kindly used. After she had discussed with him about his kindred and method of life, and found his answers ingenuous, she ordered him some cast-off garments, and that he should be cleaned, and appear like a servant in the house. Then she went to her parents and gave them her opinion of this stranger, which pleased them well, saying, "He looks like a serviceable fellow to do kitchen drudgery, run on errands, clean the shoes, and do such other things as the rest of the servants think beneath them." By this he was confirmed in his place, and a flock bed prepared in the garret for him. These conditions pleased him, and he showed great diligence in the work, rising early and sitting up late, leaving nothing undone that he could do. But his being mostly under the cook-maid, she gave him sour sauce to these little sweets; for she, being of a morose temper, used her authority beyond reason, so that to keep in the family he had many a broken head, bearing it patiently; and the more he tried with good words to dissuade her from her cruelty, the more she insulted him, and not only abused him, but frequently complained against him, endeavoring to get him turned out of his service. But Mrs. Alice, hearing of her usage, interposed in his favor, so that she should not prevail against him.

This was not the only misery he suffered, for, lying in a place for so long time unfrequented, such abundance of rats and mice had bred there that they were almost as troublesome by night as the cook was by day, running over his face and disturbing him with their squeaking, so that he knew not what to think of his condition, or how to mend it. After many disquieting thoughts, he at last comforted himself with the hope that the cook might soon marry, or die, or quit her service; and as for the rats and mice, a cat would be an effectual remedy against them. Soon after, a merchant came to dinner, and when it rained exceedingly, stayed all night. Whittington having cleaned his shoes and presented them at his chamber door, he gave him a penny. This stock the boy improved, when, going along the street of an errand, he saw a woman with a cat under her arm; so he desired to know the price of it. The woman praised it for a good mouser and told him sixpence; but he declaring that a penny was all his stock, she let him have it. He brought it home and kept it in a box all day, lest the cook should kill it if it strayed into the kitchen; and at night he set it to work for its living. Puss delivered him from one plague, but the other remained, though not for many years.

It was the custom with the worthy merchant, Mr. Hugh Fitz-Warren, that God might give him a greater blessing to his endeavors, to call all his servants together when he sent out a ship and cause everyone to venture something in it, to

try their fortune, for which they were to pay nothing for freight or custom.

Now all but Whittington appeared, and brought things according to their abilities; but Mrs. Alice being by, and supposing that poverty made him decline coming, she ordered him to be called, on which he made several excuses. However, being constrained to come, he fell upon his knees, desiring them not to jeer at a poor simple fellow in expectation that he was going to turn merchant, since all that he could lay claim to as his own was but a poor cat, which he had bought for one penny that had been given him for cleaning shoes, and which had much befriended him in keeping the rats and mice from him. Upon this Mrs. Alice proffered to lay something down for him; but her father told her the custom, it must be his own which he ventured, and ordered him to fetch his cat, which he did, but with great reluctance, fancying nothing could come of it, and with some tears delivered the animal to the master of the ship, which was called the *Unicorn*, and was to sail down to Blackwall, in order to proceed on her voyage.

The cook-maid, who little thought how advantageous Whittington's cat would prove, when she did not scold at him, would jeer him about his grand adventure, and led him such a life that he grew weary of enduring it, and, little expecting what ensued, resolved rather to try Dame Fortune than live in such great torment; and so, having packed up his bundle over night, got out early on All Hallows' Day, intending to ramble the country. But as he went through Moorfields, he began to have pensive thoughts, and his resolutions began to fail. However, on he went to Holloway, and sat down to consider the matter, when, on a sudden, Bow Bells began to ring a merry peal. He, listening, fancied they called him back from his intended journey and promised him good fortune, imagining they expressed—

> Turn again, Whittington
> Lord Mayor of London.

This was a happy thought for him, as it made so great an impression on him that, finding it early, and that he might be back before the family were stirring, he delayed not; and all things answered his expectation, for, having left the door ajar, he crept softly in and got to his usual drudgery.

During this time the ship in which the cat was, by contrary winds, was driven on the coast of Barbary, inhabited by the Moors, unknown to the English; but finding the people courteous, the Master and Factor traded with them; so, bringing their wares of sundry sorts upon deck and opening them, they pleased them so well that the news was carried to the king, who sent for patterns, with which he was so pleased that he sent for the Factor to come to his palace. Their entertainment, according to custom, was on the floor, covered with carpets interwoven with gold and silver, whereon they sat crosslegged. This kind of table was no sooner covered with various dishes but the scent drew together a great number of rats and mice, who devoured all that came in the way; which surprised the Factor, who asked the nobles if these vermin were not offensive.

"Oh," said they, "His Majesty would give half his revenue to be freed from them, for they are not only offensive at his table, but his chamber and bed are so troubled with them that he is always watched for fear of mischief." The Factor then, remembering Whittington's cat, and rejoicing at the occasion, told them that he had a English beast in the ship that would rid all the Court of them quickly. The king, overjoyed at the good news, and being anxious to be freed from those mice which so much spoiled his pleasure, desired to see this surprising creature, saying, "For such a thing I will load your ship with gold, diamonds, and pearls."

This large offer made the Master endeavor the more to enhance the cat's merits, saying, "She is the most admirable creature in the world, and I cannot spare her, for she keeps my ship clear of them, otherwise they would destroy all my goods." But His Majesty would take no denial, saying, "No price shall part us." The cat being sent for, and the tables spread, the mice came as before. Then, she being set on the table, she fell to immediately and killed them all in a trice. Then she came purring and curling up her tail to the king and queen, as if she asked a reward for her service; whilst they admired her, protesting it was the finest diversion they had ever seen.

The Moorish king was so pleased with the cat, especially when the Master told him she was with young and would stock the whole country, that he gave ten times more for the cat than all the freight besides. So they sailed with a fair wind and arrived safe at Blackwall, being the richest ship that ever came into England. The Master, taking the cabinet of jewels with him, they being too rich a prize to be left on board, presented his bill of lading to Fitz-Warren, who praised God for such a prosperous voyage. But when he called all his servants to give each his due, the Master showed him the cabinet of jewels and pearls, the sight of which much surprised him. But on being told it was all for Whittington's cat, he said, "God forbid that I should deprive him of one farthing of it." And so he sent for him by the title of Mr. Whittington, who was then in the kitchen cleaning pots and spits.

Being told he must come to his master, he made several excuses; but being urged to go, he at length came to the door, and there stood scringing and scraping, scrupling to enter, till the merchant commanded him in and ordered a chair to be immediately set for him; on which he, thinking they intended to make sport with him, fell on his knees, and with tears in his eyes besought them not to mock a simple fellow who meant none of them any harm. Mr. Fitz-Warren, raising him up, said, "Indeed, Mr. Whittington, we are serious with you, for in estate at this instant you are an abler man than myself"; and then gave him the vast riches, which amounted to three hundred thousand pounds.

At length, being persuaded to believe, he fell upon his knees and praised Almighty God, who had vouchsafed to behold so poor a creature in the midst of his misery. Then, turning to his master, he laid his riches at his feet; but he said, "No, Mr. Whittington, God forbid I should take so much as a ducat from you; may it be a comfort to you." Then he turned to Mrs. Alice, but she also refused it. Upon which, bowing low, he said unto her, "Madam, whenever you please to make choice of a husband, I will make you the greatest fortune in the world."

Upon this he began to distribute his bounty to his fellow servants, giving even his mortal enemy the cook one hundred pounds for her portion. When she said she had acted in passion, he freely forgave her. He also distributed his bounty very plentifully to all the ship's crew.

Upon this change, the haberdashers, tailors, and seamstresses were set to work to make Mr. Whittington's clothes, all things answerable to his fortune. Being dressed, he appeared a very comely person, insomuch that Mrs. Alice began to lay her eyes upon him. Now her father, seeing this, intended a match for them, looking upon him to be a fortunate man. He also took him to the Royal Exchange, to see the customs of the merchants, where he was no sooner known than they came to welcome him into their society. Soon after, a match was proposed between him and his master's daughter, when he excused himself on account of the meanness of his birth, but that objection being removed by his present worth, it was soon agreed on, and the Lord Mayor and Aldermen invited to the wedding.

After the honeymoon was over, his father-in-law asked him what employment he would follow. Whereupon he replied he should think of that of a merchant. So they joined together in partnership, and both grew immensely rich.

Though fortune had thus bountifully smiled on the subject of our history, he was far from proud, yet merry, which made his company and acquaintance courted by all. In a short time he was nominated Sheriff of London and thereafter Lord Mayor, in which office he behaved with such justice and prudence that he was chosen to it twice afterward.

6.

The Story of Webster

by P. G. WODEHOUSE

Prolific P. G. Wodehouse is accepted as one of the greatest humorous novelists of his era. Born in England in the 1880's, and presently residing on a Long Island estate, his earliest job was in a London bank; to our good fortune, he shortly gave up high finance to become a free-lance writer. The creation of Jeeves, a "gentleman's gentleman" (*The Inimitable Jeeves,* 1924), assured his position as a humorist; he maintained this reputation with a succession of short stories, sketches, librettos, and musical comedies, as well as sparkling novels. "The Story of Webster" shows what may happen when a cat becomes an unwanted member of a household—and takes over.

"Cats are not dogs!"

There is only one place where you can hear good things like that thrown off quite casually in the general run of conversation, and that is the bar-parlour of the Anglers' Rest. It was there, as we sat grouped about the fire, that a thoughtful Pint of Bitter had made the statement just recorded.

Although the talk up to this point had been dealing with Einstein's Theory of Relativity, we readily adjusted our minds to cope with the new topic. Regular attendance at the nightly session at which Mr. Mulliner presides with such unfailing dignity and geniality tends to produce mental nimbleness. In our little circle I have known an argument on the Final Destination of the Soul to change inside forty seconds into one concerning the best method of preserving the juiciness of bacon fat.

"Cats," proceeded the Pint of Bitter, "are selfish. A man waits on a cat hand and foot for weeks, humouring its lightest whim, and then it goes and leaves him flat because it has found a place down the road where the fish is more frequent."

"What I've got against cats," said a Lemon Sour, speaking feelingly, as one brooding on a private grievance, "is their unreliability. They lack candour and are not square shooters. You get your cat and you call him Thomas or George, as the case may be. So far so good. Then one morning you wake up and find a litter in the cat box and you have to reopen the whole matter, approaching it from an entirely different angle."

"If you want to know what's the trouble with cats," said a red-faced man with glassy eyes, who had been rapping on the table for his fourth whisky, "they've got no tact. That's what's the trouble with them. I remember a friend of mine had a cat. Made quite a pet of that cat, he did. And what occurred? What was the outcome? One night he came home rather late and was feeling for the keyhole with his corkscrew; and, believe me or not, his cat selected that precise moment to jump on the back of his neck out of a tree. No tact."

Mr. Mulliner shook his head.

"I grant you all this," he said, "but still, in my opinion, you have not got quite to the root of the matter. The real objection to the great majority of cats is their unsufferable air of superiority. Cats, as a class, have never completely got over the snootiness caused by the fact that in Ancient Egypt they were worshipped as gods. This makes them too prone to set themselves up as critics and censors of the frail and erring human beings whose lot they share. They stare rebukingly.

They view with concern. And on a sensitive man this often has the worst effects, inducing an inferiority complex of the gravest kind. It is odd that the conversation should have taken this turn," said Mr. Mulliner, sipping his hot Scotch and lemon, "for I was thinking only this afternoon of the rather strange case of my cousin Edward's son, Lancelot."

"I knew a cat—" began a Small Bass.

My cousin Edward's son, Lancelot (said Mr. Mulliner) was, at the time of which I speak, a comely youth of some twenty-five summers. Orphaned at an early age, he had been brought up in the home of his Uncle Theodore, the saintly Dean of Bolsover; and it was a great shock to that good man when Lancelot, on attaining his majority, wrote from London to inform him that he had taken a studio in Bott Street, Chelsea, and proposed to remain in the metropolis and become an artist.

The Dean's opinion of artists was low. As a prominent member of the Bolsover Watch Committee, it had recently been his distasteful duty to be present at a private showing of the super-super film, "Palettes of Passion"; and he replied to his nephew's communication with a vibrant letter in which he emphasized the grievous pain it gave him to think that one of his flesh and blood should deliberately be embarking on a career which must inevitably lead sooner or later to the painting of Russian princesses lying on divans in the semi-nude with their arms round tame jaguars. He urged Lancelot to return and become a curate while there was yet time.

But Lancelot was firm. He deplored the rift between himself and a relative whom he had always respected; but he was dashed if he meant to go back to an environment where his individuality had been stifled and his soul confined in chains. For four years there was silence between uncle and nephew.

During these years Lancelot had made progress in his chosen profession. At the time at which this story opens, his prospects seemed bright. He was painting the portrait of Brenda, only daughter of Mr. and Mrs. B. B. Carberry-Pirbright, of 11 Maxton Square, South Kensington, which meant thirty pounds in his sock on delivery. He had learned to cook eggs and bacon. He had practically mastered the ukulele. And, in addition, he was engaged to be married to a fearless young *vers libre* poetess of the name of Gladys Bingley, better known as The Sweet Singer of Garbidge Mews, Fulham—a charming girl who looked like a pen-wiper.

It seemed to Lancelot that life was very full and beautiful. He lived joyously in the present, giving no thought to the past.

But how true it is that the past is inextricably mixed up with the present and that we can never tell when it may not spring some delayed bomb beneath our feet. One afternoon, as he sat making a few small alterations in the portrait of Brenda Carberry-Pirbright, his fiancée entered.

He had been expecting her to call, for today she was going off for a three weeks' holiday to the South of France, and she had promised to look in on her way to the station. He laid down his brush and gazed at her with a yearning affection, thinking for the thousandth time how he worshipped every spot of ink on her nose. Standing there in the doorway with her bobbed hair sticking out in every direction like a golliwog's she made a picture that seemed to speak to his very depths.

"Hullo, Reptile!" he said lovingly.

"What ho, Worm!" said Gladys, maidenly devotion shining

through the monocle which she wore in her left eye. "I can stay just half an hour."

"Oh, well, half an hour soon passes," said Lancelot. "What's that you've got there?"

"A letter, ass. What did you think it was?"

"Where did you get it?"

"I found the postman outside."

Lancelot took the envelope from her and examined it. "Gosh!" he said.

"What's the matter?"

"It's from my Uncle Theodore."

"I didn't know you had an Uncle Theodore."

"Of course I have. I've had him for years."

"What's he writing to you about?"

"If you'll kindly keep quiet for two seconds, if you know how," said Lancelot, "I'll tell you."

And in a clear voice which, like that of all Mulliners, however distant from the main branch, was beautifully modulated, he read as follows:

"The Deanery,
"Bolsover,
"Wilts.

"My Dear Lancelot,

"As you have, no doubt, already learned from your *Church Times,* I have been offered and have accepted the vacant Bishopric of Bongo-Bongo in West Africa. I sail immediately to take up my new duties, which I trust will be blessed.

"In these circumstances, it becomes necessary for me to find a good home for my cat Webster. It is, alas, out of the question that he should accompany me, as the rigours of the climate and the lack of essential comforts might well sap a constitution which has never been robust.

"I am dispatching him, therefore, to your address, my dear boy, in a straw-lined hamper, in the full confidence that you will prove a kindly and conscientious host.

> "With cordial good wishes,
> "Your affectionate uncle,
> "Theodore Bongo-Bongo."

For some moments after he had finished reading this communication, a thoughtful silence prevailed in the studio. Finally Gladys spoke.

"Of all the nerve!" she said. "I wouldn't do it."

"Why not?"

"What do you want with a cat?"

Lancelot reflected.

"It is true," he said, "that, given a free hand, I would prefer not to have my studio turned into a cattery or cat-bin. But consider the special circumstances. Relations between Uncle Theodore and self have for the last few years been a bit strained. In fact, you might say we had definitely parted brass-rags. It looks to me as if he were coming round. I should describe this letter as more or less what you might call an olive-branch. If I lush this cat up satisfactorily, shall I not be in a position later on to make a swift touch?"

"He is rich, this bean?" said Gladys, interested.

"Extremely."

"Then," said Gladys, "consider my objections withdrawn. A good stout cheque from a grateful cat-fancier would undoubtedly come in very handy. We might be able to get married this year."

"Exactly," said Lancelot. "A pretty loathsome prospect, of course, but still, as we've arranged to do it, the sooner we get it over, the better, what?"

"Absolutely."

"Then that's settled. I accept custody of cat."

"It's the only thing to do," said Gladys. "Meanwhile, can you lend me a comb? Have you such a thing in your bedroom?"

"What do you want with a comb?"

"I got some soup in my hair at lunch. I won't be a minute."

She hurried out, and Lancelot, taking up the letter again, found that he had omitted to read a continuation of it on the back page.

It was to the following effect:

"P.S. In establishing Webster in your home, I am actuated by another motive than the simple desire to see to it that my faithful friend and companion is adequately provided for.

"From both a moral and an educative standpoint, I am convinced that Webster's society will prove of inestimable value to you. His advent, indeed, I venture to hope, will be a turning point in your life. Thrown, as you must be, incessantly among loose and immoral Bohemians, you will find in this cat an example of upright conduct which cannot but act as an antidote to the poison cup of temptation which is, no doubt, hourly pressed to your lips.

"P.P.S. Cream only at midday, and fish not more than three times a week."

He was reading these words for the second time, when the front door-bell rang and he found a man on the steps with a hamper. A discreet mew from within revealed its contents, and Lancelot, carrying it into the studio, cut the strings.

"Hi!" he bellowed, going to the door.

"What's up?" shrieked his betrothed from above.

"The cat's come."

"All right. I'll be down in a jiffy."

Lancelot returned to the studio.

"What ho, Webster!" he said cheerily. "How's the boy?"

The cat did not reply. It was sitting with bent head, performing that wash and brush up which a journey by rail renders so necessary.

In order to facilitate these toilet operations, it had raised its left leg and was holding it rigidly in the air. And there flashed into Lancelot's mind an old superstition handed on to him, for what it was worth, by one of the nurses of his infancy. If, this woman had said, you creep up to a cat when its leg is in the air and give it a pull, then you make a wish and your wish comes true in thirty days.

It was a pretty fancy, and it seemed to Lancelot that the theory might as well be put to the test. He advanced warily, therefore, and was in the act of extending his fingers for the pull, when Webster, lowering the leg, turned and raised his eyes.

He looked at Lancelot. And suddenly with sickening force, there came to Lancelot the realization of the unpardonable liberty he had been about to take.

Until this moment, though the postscript to his uncle's letter should have warned him, Lancelot Mulliner had had no

suspicion of what manner of cat this was that he had taken into his home. Now, for the first time, he saw him steadily and saw him whole.

Webster was very large and very black and very composed. He conveyed the impression of being a cat of deep reserves. Descendant of a long line of ecclesiastical ancestors who had conducted their decorous courtships beneath the shadow of cathedrals and on the back walls of bishops' palaces, he had that exquisite poise which one sees in high dignitaries of the church. His eyes were clear and steady, and seemed to pierce to the very roots of the young man's soul, filling him with a sense of guilt.

Once, long ago, in his hot childhood, Lancelot, spending his summer holidays at the deanery, had been so far carried away by ginger-beer and original sin as to plug a senior canon in the leg with his air-gun—only to discover, on turning, that a visiting archdeacon had been a spectator of the entire incident from his immediate rear. As he had felt then, when meeting the archdeacon's eye, so did he feel now as Webster's gaze played silently upon him.

Webster, it is true, had not actually raised his eyebrows. But this, Lancelot felt, was simply because he hadn't any.

He backed, blushing.

"Sorry!" he muttered.

There was a pause. Webster continued his steady scrutiny. Lancelot edged towards the door.

"Er—excuse me—just a moment . . ." he mumbled. And, sidling from the room, he ran distractedly upstairs.

"I say," said Lancelot.

"Now what?" asked Gladys.

"Have you finished with the mirror?"

"Why?"

"Well, I—er—I thought," said Lancelot, "that I might as well have a shave."

The girl looked at him, astonished.

"Shave? Why, you shaved only the day before yesterday."

"I know. But, all the same . . . I mean to say, it seems only respectful. That cat, I mean."

"What about him?"

"Well, he seems to expect it, somehow. Nothing actually said, don't you know, but you could tell by his manner. I thought a quick shave and perhaps change into my blue serge suit—"

"He's probably thirsty. Why don't you give him some milk?"

"Could one, do you think?" said Lancelot doubtfully. "I mean, I hardly seem to know him well enough." He paused. "I say, old girl," he went on, with a touch of hesitation.

"Hullo?"

"I know you won't mind my mentioning it, but you've got a few spots of ink on your nose."

"Of course I have. I always have spots of ink on my nose."

"Well . . . you don't think . . . a quick scrub with a bit of pumice-stone . . . I mean to say, you know how important first impressions are . . ."

The girl stared.

"Lancelot Mulliner," she said, 'if you think I'm going to skin my nose to the bone just to please a mangy cat—"

"Sh!" cried Lancelot, in agony.

"Here, let me go down and look at him," said Gladys petulantly.

As they re-entered the studio, Webster was gazing with an air of quiet distaste at an illustration from *La Vie Parisienne* which adorned one of the walls. Lancelot tore it down hastily.

Gladys looked at Webster in an unfriendly way.

"So that's the blighter!"

"Sh!"

"If you want to know what I think," said Gladys, "that cat's been living too high. Doing himself a dashed sight too well. You'd better cut his rations down a bit."

In substance, her criticism was not unjustified. Certainly, there was about Webster more than a suspicion of *embonpoint*. He had that air of portly well-being which we associate with those who dwell in cathedral closes. But Lancelot winced uncomfortably. He had so hoped that Gladys would make a good impression, and here she was, starting right off by saying the tactless thing.

He longed to explain to Webster that it was only her way; that in the Bohemian circles of which she was an ornament genial chaff of a personal order was accepted and, indeed, relished. But it was too late. The mischief had been done. Webster turned in a pointed manner and withdrew silently behind the chesterfield.

Gladys, all unconscious, was making preparations for departure.

"Well, bung-oh," she said lightly. "See you in three weeks. I suppose you and that cat'll both be out on the tiles the moment my back's turned."

"Please! Please!" moaned Lancelot. "Please!"

He had caught sight of the tip of a black tail protruding from behind the chesterfield. It was twitching slightly, and Lancelot could read it like a book. With a sickening sense of dismay, he knew that Webster had formed a snap judgement of his fiancée and condemned her as frivolous and unworthy.

It was some ten days later that Bernard Worple, the neo-Vorticist sculptor, lunching at the Puce Ptarmigan, ran into

Rodney Scollop, the powerful young surrealist. And after talking for a while of their art—

"What's all this I hear about Lancelot Mulliner?" asked Worple. "There's a wild story going about that he was seen shaved in the middle of the week. Nothing in it, I suppose?"

Scollop looked grave. He had been on the point of mentioning Lancelot himself, for he loved the lad and was deeply exercised about him.

"It is perfectly true," he said.

"It sounds incredible."

Scollop leaned forward. His fine face was troubled.

"Shall I tell you something, Worple?"

"What?"

"I know for an absolute fact," said Scollop, "that Lancelot Mulliner now shaves every morning."

Worple pushed aside the spaghetti which he was wreathing about him and through the gap stared at his companion.

"Every morning?"

"Every single morning. I looked in on him myself the other day, and there he was, neatly dressed in blue serge and shaved to the core. And, what is more, I got the distinct impression that he had used talcum powder afterwards."

"You don't mean that!"

"I do. And shall I tell you something else? There was a book lying open on the table. He tried to hide it, but he wasn't quick enough. It was one of those etiquette books!"

"An etiquette book!"

"*Polite Behaviour*, by Constance, Lady Bodbank."

Worple unwound a stray tendril of spaghetti from about his left ear. He was deeply agitated. Like Scollop, he loved Lancelot.

"He'll be dressing for dinner next!" he exclaimed.

"I have every reason to believe," said Scollop gravely, "that he does dress for dinner. At any rate, a man closely resembling him was seen furtively buying three stiff collars and a black tie at Hope Brothers in the King's Road last Tuesday."

Worple pushed his chair back, and rose. His manner was determined.

"Scollop," he said, "we are friends of Mulliner's, you and I. It is evident from what you tell me that subversive influences are at work and that never has he needed our friendship more. Shall we not go round and see him immediately?"

"It was what I was about to suggest myself," said Rodney Scollop.

Twenty minutes later they were in Lancelot's studio, and with a significant glance Scollop drew his companion's notice to their host's appearance. Lancelot Mulliner was neatly, even foppishly, dressed in blue serge with creases down the trouserlegs, and his chin, Worple saw with a pang, gleamed smoothly in the afternoon light.

At the sight of his friends' cigars, Lancelot exhibited unmistakable concern.

"You don't mind throwing those away, I'm sure," he said pleadingly.

Rodney Scollop drew himself up a little haughtily.

"And since when," he asked, "have the best fourpenny cigars in Chelsea not been good enough for you?"

Lancelot hastened to soothe him.

"It isn't me," he exclaimed. "It's Webster. My cat. I happen to know he objects to tobacco smoke. I had to give up my pipe in deference to his views."

Bernard Worple snorted.

"Are you trying to tell us," he sneered, "that Lancelot

Mulliner allows himself to be dictated to by a blasted cat?"

"Hush!" cried Lancelot, trembling. "If you knew how he disapproves of strong language!"

"Where is this cat?" asked Rodney Scollop. "Is that the animal?" he said, pointing out of the window to where, in the yard, a tough-looking Tom with tattered ears stood mewing in a hard-boiled way out of the corner of its mouth.

"Good heavens, no!" said Lancelot. "That is an alley cat which comes round here from time to time to lunch at the dustbin. Webster is quite different. Webster has a natural dignity and repose of manner. Webster is a cat who prides himself on always being well turned out and whose high principles and lofty ideals shine from his eyes like beacon-fires . . ." And then suddenly, with an abrupt change of manner, Lancelot broke down and in a low voice added: "Curse him! Curse him! Curse him! Curse him!"

Worple looked at Scollop. Scollop looked at Worple.

"Come, old man," said Scollop, laying a gentle hand on Lancelot's bowed shoulder. "We are your friends. Confide in us."

"Tell us all," said Worple. "What's the matter?"

Lancelot uttered a bitter, mirthless laugh.

"You want to know what's the matter? Listen, then. I'm cat-pecked!"

"Cat-pecked?"

"You've heard of men being hen-pecked, haven't you?" said Lancelot with a touch of irritation. "Well, I'm cat-pecked."

And in broken accents he told his story. He sketched the history of his association with Webster from the latter's first entry into the studio. Confident now that the animal was not within earshot, he unbosomed himself without reserve.

"It's something in the beast's eye," he said in a shaking voice. "Something hypnotic. He casts a spell upon me. He gazes at me and disapproves. Little by little, bit by bit, I am degenerating under his influence from a wholesome, self-respecting artist into . . . well, I don't know what you would call it. Suffice it to say that I have given up smoking, that I have ceased to wear carpet slippers and go about without a collar, that I never dream of sitting down to my frugal evening meal without dressing, and"—he choked—"I have sold my ukulele."

"Not that!" said Worple, paling.

"Yes," said Lancelot. "I felt he considered it frivolous." There was a long silence.

"Mulliner," said Scollop, "this is more serious than I had supposed. We must brood upon your case."

"It may be possible," said Worple, "to find a way out." Lancelot shook his head hopelessly.

"There is no way out. I have explored every avenue. The only thing that could possibly free me from this intolerable bondage would be if once—just once—I could catch that cat unbending. If once—merely once—it would lapse in my presence from its austere dignity for but a single instant, I feel that the spell would be broken. But what hope is there of that?" cried Lancelot passionately. "You were pointing just now to that alley cat in the yard. There stands one who has strained every nerve and spared no effort to break down Webster's inhuman self-control. I have heard that animal say things to him which you would think no cat with red blood in its veins would suffer for an instant. And Webster merely looks at him like a Suffragan Bishop eyeing an erring choir-boy and turns his head and falls into a refreshing sleep."

He broke off with a dry sob. Worple, always an optimist, attempted in his kindly way to minimize the tragedy.

"Ah, well," he said. "It's bad, of course, but still, I suppose there is no actual harm in shaving and dressing for dinner and so on. Many great artists . . . Whistler, for example—"

"Wait!" cried Lancelot. "You have not heard the worst."

He rose feverishly, and, going to the easel, disclosed the portrait of Brenda Carberry-Pirbright.

"Take a look at that," he said, "and tell me what you think of her."

His two friends surveyed the face before them in silence. Miss Carberry-Pirbright was a young woman of prim and glacial aspect. One sought in vain for her reasons for wanting to have her portrait painted. It would be a most unpleasant thing to have about any house.

Scollop broke the silence.

"Friend of yours?"

"I can't stand the sight of her," said Lancelot vehemently.

"Then," said Scollop, "I may speak frankly. I think she's a pill."

"A blister," said Worple.

"A boil and a disease," said Scollop, summing up.

Lancelot laughed hackingly.

"You have described her to a nicety. She stands for everything most alien to my artist soul. She gives me a pain in the neck. I'm going to marry her."

"What!" cried Scollop.

"But you're going to marry Gladys Bingley," said Worple.

"Webster thinks not," said Lancelot bitterly. "At their first meeting he weighed Gladys in the balance and found her wanting. And the moment he saw Brenda Carberry-Pirbright he stuck his tail up at right angles, uttered a cordial gargle, and rubbed his head against her leg. Then, turning, he looked at me. I could read that glance. I knew what was in his mind. From that moment he has been doing everything in his power to arrange the match."

"But, Mulliner," said Worple, always eager to point out the bright side, "why should this girl want to marry a wretched, scrubby, hard-up footler like you? Have courage, Mulliner. It is simply a question of time before you repel and sicken her."

Lancelot shook his head.

"No," he said. "You speak like a true friend, Worple, but you do not understand. Old Ma Carberry-Pirbright, this exhibit's mother, who chaperons her at the sittings, discovered at an early date my relationship to my Uncle Theodore, who, as you know, has got it in gobs. She knows well enough that some day I shall be a rich man. She used to know my Uncle Theodore when he was Vicar of St. Botolph's in Knightsbridge, and from the very first she assumed towards me the repellent chumminess of an old family friend. She was always trying to lure me to her At Homes, her Sunday luncheons, her little dinners. Once she actually suggested that I should escort her and her beastly daughter to the Royal Academy."

He laughed bitterly. The mordant witticisms of Lancelot Mulliner at the expense of the Royal Academy were quoted from Tite Street in the south to Holland Park in the north and eastward as far as Bloomsbury.

"To all these overtures," resumed Lancelot, "I remained firmly unresponsive. My attitude was from the start one of frigid aloofness. I did not actually say in so many words that I would rather be dead in a ditch than at one of her At Homes, but my manner indicated it. And I was just beginning to think I had choked her off when in crashed Webster and upset everything. Do you know how many times I have been to that infernal house in the last week? Five. Webster seemed to wish it. I tell you, I am a lost man."

He buried his face in his hands. Scollop touched Worple on the arm, and together the two men stole silently out.

"Bad!" said Worple.

"Very bad," said Scollop.

"It seems incredible."

"Oh, no. Cases of this kind are, alas, by no means uncommon among those who, like Mulliner, possess to a marked degree the highly-strung, ultra-sensitive artistic temperament. A friend of mine, a rhythmical interior decorator, once rashly consented to put his aunt's parrot up at his studio while she was away visiting friends in the north of England. She was a woman of strong evangelical views, which the bird had imbibed from her. It had a way of putting its head on one side, making a noise like someone drawing a cork from a bottle, and asking my friend if he was saved. To cut a long story short, I happened to call on him a month later and he had installed a harmonium in his studio and was singing hymns, ancient and modern, in a rich tenor, while the parrot, standing on one leg on its perch, took the bass. A very sad affair. We were all much upset about it."

Worple shuddered.

"You appall me, Scollop! Is there nothing we can do?"

Rodney Scollop considered for a moment.

"We might wire Gladys Bingley to come home at once. She might possibly reason with the unhappy man. A woman's gentle influence . . . Yes, we could do that. Look in at the post office on your way home and send Gladys a telegram. I'll owe you for my half of it."

In the studio they had left, Lancelot Mulliner was staring dumbly at a black shape which had just entered the room. He had the appearance of a man with his back to the wall.

"No!" he was crying. "No! I'm dashed if I do!"

Webster continued to look at him.

"Why should I?" demanded Lancelot weakly.

Webster's gaze did not flicker.

"Oh, all right," said Lancelot sullenly.

He passed from the room with leaden feet, and, proceeding upstairs, changed into morning clothes and a top hat. Then, with a gardenia in his buttonhole, he made his way to 11 Maxton Square, where Mrs. Carberry-Pirbright was giving one of her intimate little teas ("just a few friends") to meet Clara Throckmorton Stooge, authoress of *A Strong Man's Kiss*.

Gladys Bingley was lunching at her hotel in Antibes when Worple's telegram arrived. It occasioned her the gravest concern.

Exactly what it was all about, she was unable to gather, for emotion had made Bernard Worple rather incoherent. There were moments, reading it, when she fancied that Lancelot had met with a serious accident; others when the solution seemed to be that he had sprained his brain to such an extent that rival lunatic asylums were competing eagerly for his custom; others, again, when Worple appeared to be suggesting that he had gone into partnership with his cat to start a harem. But one fact emerged clearly. Her loved one was in serious trouble of some kind, and his best friends were agreed that only her immediate return could save him.

Gladys did not hesitate. Within half an hour of the receipt of the telegram she had packed her trunk, removed a piece of asparagus from her right eyebrow, and was negotiating for accommodation on the first train going north.

Arriving in London, her first impulse was to go straight to Lancelot. But a natural feminine curiosity urged her, before doing so, to call upon Bernard Worple and have light thrown on some of the more abstruse passages in the telegram.

Worple, in his capacity of author, may have tended towards obscurity, but, when confining himself to the spoken word, he told a plain story well and clearly. Five minutes of his society enabled Gladys to obtain a firm grasp on the salient facts, and there appeared on her face that grim, tight-lipped expression which is seen only on the faces of fiancées who have come back from a short holiday to discover that their dear one has been straying in their absence from the straight and narrow path.

"Brenda Carberry-Pirbright, eh?" said Gladys, with ominous calm. "I'll give him Brenda Carberry-Pirbright! My gosh, if one can't go off to Antibes for the merest breather without having one's betrothed getting it up his nose and starting to act like a Mormon Elder, it begins to look a pretty tough world for a girl."

Kind-hearted Bernard Worple did his best.

"I blame the cat," he said. "Lancelot, to my mind, is more sinned against than sinning. I consider him to be acting under undue influence or duress."

"How like a man!" said Gladys. "Shoving it all off on to an innocent cat!"

"Lancelot says that it has a sort of something in its eye."

"Well, when I meet Lancelot," said Gladys, "he'll find that I have a sort of something in my eye."

She went out, breathing flame quietly through her nostrils.

Worple, saddened, heaved a sigh and resumed his neo-Vorticist sculpting.

It was some five minutes later that Gladys, passing through Maxton Square on her way to Bott Street, stopped suddenly in her tracks. The sight she had seen was enough to make any fiancée do so.

Along the pavement leading to Number Eleven two figures were advancing. Or three, if you counted a morose-looking dog of a semi-Dachshund nature which preceded them, attached to a leash. One of the figures was that of Lancelot Mulliner, natty in grey herring-bone tweed and a new Homburg hat. It was he who held the leash. The other Gladys recognized from the portrait which she had seen on Lancelot's easel as that modern Du Barry, that notorious wrecker of homes and breaker-up of love-nests, Brenda Carberry-Pirbright.

The next moment they had mounted the steps of Number Eleven, and had gone in to tea, possibly with a little music.

It was perhaps an hour and a half later that Lancelot, having wrenched himself with difficulty from the lair of the Philistines, sped homeward in a swift taxi. As always after an extended *tête-à-tête* with Miss Carberry-Pirbright, he felt dazed and bewildered, as if he had been swimming in a sea of glue and had swallowed a good deal of it. All he could think of clearly was that he wanted a drink and that the materials for that drink were in the cupboard behind the chesterfield in his studio.

He paid the cab and charged in with his tongue rattling dryly against his front teeth. And there before him was Gladys Bingley, whom he had supposed far, far away.

"You!" exclaimed Lancelot.

"Yes, me!" said Gladys.

Her long vigil had not helped to restore the girl's equanimity. Since arriving at the studio she had had leisure to tap her foot three thousand, one hundred and forty-two times on the carpet, and the number of bitter smiles which had flitted across her face was nine hundred and eleven. She was about ready for the battle of the century.

She rose and faced him, all the woman in her flashing from her eyes.

"Well, you Casanova!" she said.

"You who?" said Lancelot.

"Don't say 'Yoo-hoo!' to me!" cried Gladys. "Keep that for your Brenda Carberry-Pirbrights. Yes, I know all about it, Lancelot Don Juan Henry the Eighth Mulliner! I saw you with her just now. I hear that you and she are inseparable. Bernard Worple says you said you were going to marry her."

"You mustn't believe everything a neo-Vorticist sculptor tells you," quavered Lancelot.

"I'll bet you're going back to dinner there tonight," said Gladys.

She had spoken at a venture, basing the charge purely on a possessive cock of the head which she had noticed in Brenda Carberry-Pirbright at their recent encounter. There, she had said to herself at the time, had gone a girl who was about to invite—or had just invited—Lancelot Mulliner to dine quietly and take her to the pictures afterwards. But the shot went home. Lancelot hung his head.

"There was some talk of it," he admitted.

"Ah!" exclaimed Gladys.

Lancelot's eyes were haggard.

"I don't want to go," he pleaded. "Honestly I don't. But Webster insists."

"Webster!"

"Yes, Webster. If I attempt to evade the appointment, he will sit in front of me and look at me."

"Tchah!"

"Well, he will. Ask him for yourself."

Gladys tapped her foot six times in rapid succession on the carpet, bringing the total to three thousand, one hundred and forty-eight. Her manner had changed and was now danger-ously calm.

"Lancelot Mulliner," she said, "you have your choice. Me, on the one hand, Brenda Carberry-Pirbright on the other. I offer you a home where you will be able to smoke in bed, spill the ashes on the floor, wear pyjamas and carpet-slippers all day and shave only on Sunday mornings. From her, what have you to hope? A house in South Kensington—possibly the Brompton Road—probably with her mother living with you. A life that will be one long round of stiff collars and tight shoes, of morning-coats and top hats."

Lancelot quivered, but she went on remorselessly.

"You will be at home on alternate Thursdays, and will be expected to hand the cucumber sandwiches. Every day you will air the dog, till you become a confirmed dog-airer. You will dine out in Bayswater and go for the summer to Bournemouth or Dinard. Choose well, Lancelot Mulliner! I will leave you to think it over. But one last word. If by seven-thirty on the dot you have not presented yourself at 6A Garbidge Mews ready to take me out to dinner at the Ham and Beef, I shall know what to think and shall act accord-ingly."

And brushing the cigarette ashes from her chin, the girl strode haughtily from the room.

"Gladys!" cried Lancelot.

But she had gone.

For some minutes Lancelot Mulliner remained where he was, stunned. Then, insistently, there came to him the recollection that he had not had that drink. He rushed to the cupboard and produced the bottle. He uncorked it, and was pouring out a lavish stream, when a movement on the floor below him attracted his attention.

Webster was standing there, looking up at him. And in his eyes was that familiar expression of quiet rebuke.

"Scarcely what I have been accustomed to at the Deanery," he seemed to be saying.

Lancelot stood paralysed. The feeling of being bound hand and foot, of being caught in a snare from which there was no escape, had become more poignant than ever. The bottle fell from his nerveless fingers and rolled across the floor, spilling its contents in an amber river, but he was too heavy in spirit to notice it. With a gesture such as Job might have made on discovering a new boil, he crossed to the window and stood looking moodily out.

Then, turning with a sigh, he looked at Webster again— and, looking, stood spellbound.

The spectacle which he beheld was of a kind to stun a stronger man than Lancelot Mulliner. At first, he shrank from believing his eyes. Then, slowly, came the realization that what he saw was no mere figment of a disordered imagination. This unbelievable thing was actually happening.

Webster sat crouched upon the floor beside the widening pool of whisky. But it was not horror and disgust that had caused him to crouch. He was crouched because, crouching, he could get nearer to the stuff and obtain crisper action. His tongue was moving in and out like a piston.

And then abruptly, for one fleeting instant, he stopped

lapping and glanced up at Lancelot, and across his face there
flitted a quick smile—so genial, so intimate, so full of jovial
camaraderie, that the young man found himself automatically smiling back, and not only smiling but winking. And
in answer to that wink Webster winked, too—a whole-
hearted, roguish wink that said as plainly as if he had spoken
the words:

"How long has this been going on?"

Then with a slight hiccough he turned back to the task of
getting his quick before it soaked into the floor.

Into the murky soul of Lancelot Mulliner there poured a
sudden flood of sunshine. It was as if a great burden had
been lifted from his shoulders. The intolerable obsession of
the last two weeks had ceased to oppress him, and he felt a
free man. At the eleventh hour the reprieve had come. Webster, that seeming pillar of austere virtue, was one of the
boys, after all. Never again would Lancelot quail beneath
his eye. He had the goods on him.

Webster, like the stag at eve, had now drunk his fill. He
had left the pool of alcohol and was walking round in slow,
meditative circles. From time to time he mewed tentatively,
as if he were trying to say "British Constitution." His failure
to articulate the syllables appeared to tickle him, for at the
end of each attempt he would utter a slow, amused chuckle.
It was at about this moment that he suddenly broke into a
rhythmic dance, not unlike the old Saraband.

It was an interesting spectacle, and at any other time
Lancelot would have watched it raptly. But now he was
busy at his desk, writing a brief note to Mrs. Carberry-Pirbright, the burden of which was that if she thought he was
coming within a mile of her foul house that night or any other

night she had vastly underrated the dodging powers of Lancelot Mulliner.

And what of Webster? The Demon Rum now had him in an iron grip. A lifetime of abstinence had rendered him a ready victim to the fatal fluid. He had now reached the stage when geniality gives way to belligerence. The rather foolish smile had gone from his face, and in its stead there lowered a fighting frown. For a few moments he stood on his hind legs, looking about him for a suitable adversary: then, losing all vestiges of self-control, he ran five times round the room at a high rate of speed and, falling foul of a small footstool, attacked it with the utmost ferocity, sparing neither tooth nor claw.

But Lancelot did not see him. Lancelot was not there. Lancelot was out in Bott Street hailing a cab.

"6A Garbidge Mews, Fulham," said Lancelot to the driver.

7.

The Cat from Thebes

by ARTHUR WEIGALL

Arthur Weigall's weird tale of the cat of Thebes is no work of fiction. Weigall, a British archaeologist who lived from 1880 to 1934, spent many seasons excavating in Egypt, beginning as a 21-year-old novice working under the great Flinders Petrie. He was the author of a number of books about ancient Egypt; this tale of a mysterious feline spirit was included in a volume that he wrote shortly after the discovery of the spectacular tomb of Pharaoh Tut-ankh-Amen in 1922.

In the year 1909 Lord Carnarvon, who was then conducting excavations in the necropolis of the nobles of Thebes, discovered a hollow wooden figure of a large black cat, which was recognised, from other examples in the Cairo museum, to be the shell in which a real embalmed cat was confined. The figure looked more like a small tiger as it sat in the sunlight at the edge of the pit in which it had been discovered, glaring at us with its yellow painted eyes and bristling its yellow whiskers. Its body was covered all over with a thick coating of smooth, shining pitch, and we could not at first detect the line along which the shell had been closed after it had received the mortal remains of the sacred animal within; but we knew from experience that the joint passed completely round the figure—from the nose, over the top of the head, down the back, and along the breast—so that, when opened, the two sides would fall apart in equal halves.

The sombre figure was carried down to the Nile and across the river to my house, where, by a mistake on the part of my Egyptian servant, it was deposited in my *bedroom*. Returning home at dead of night, I here found it seated in the middle of the floor directly in my path from the door to the matches; and for some moments I was constrained to sit beside it, rubbing my shins and my head.

I rang the bell, but receiving no answer, I walked to the kitchen, where I found the servants grouped distractedly around the butler, who had been stung by a scorpion and was in the throes of that short but intense agony. Soon he passed into a state of delirium and believed himself to be pursued by a large grey cat, a fancy which did not surprise me since he had so lately assisted in carrying the figure to its ill-chosen resting-place in my bedroom.

At length I retired to bed, but the moonlight which now entered the room through the open French windows fell full upon the black figure of the cat; and for some time I lay awake watching the peculiarly weird creature as it stared past me at the wall. I estimated its age to be considerably more than three thousand years, and I tried to picture to myself the strange people who, in those distant times, had fashioned this curious coffin for a cat which had been to them half pet and half household god. A branch of a tree was swaying in the night breeze outside, and its shadow danced to and fro over the face of the cat, causing the yellow eyes to open and shut, as it were, and the mouth to grin. Once, as I was dropping off to sleep, I could have sworn that it had turned its head to look at me; and I could see the sullen expression of feline anger gathering upon its black visage as it did so. In

the distance I could hear the melancholy wails of the un-
fortunate butler imploring those around him to keep the cat
away from him, and it seemed to me that there came a
glitter into the eyes of the figure as the low cries echoed down
the passage.

At last I fell asleep, and for about an hour all was still.
Then, suddenly, a report like that of a pistol rang through
the room. I started up, and as I did so a large grey cat sprang
either from or on to the bed, leapt across my knees, dug its
claws into my hand, and dashed through the window into
the garden. At the same moment I saw by the light of the
moon that the two sides of the wooden figure had fallen
apart and were rocking themselves to a standstill upon the
floor, like two great empty shells. Between them sat the
mummified figure of a cat, the bandages which swathed it
round being ripped open at the neck, as though they had
been burst outward.

I sprang out of bed and rapidly examined the divided
shell; and it seemed to me that the humidity in the air here
on the bank of the Nile had expanded the wood which had
rested in the dry desert so long, and had caused the two
halves to burst apart with the loud noise which I had heard.
Then, going to the window, I scanned the moonlit garden;
and there in the middle of the pathway I saw, not the grey
cat which had scratched me, but my own pet tabby, standing
with arched back and bristling fur, glaring into the bushes,
as though she saw ten feline devils therein.

I will leave the reader to decide whether the grey cat was
the malevolent spirit which, after causing me to break my
shins and my butler to be stung by a scorpion, had burst its
way through the bandages and woodwork and had fled into
the darkness; or whether the torn embalming cloths repre-

sented the natural destructive work of Time, and the grey cat was a night-wanderer which had strayed into my room and had been frightened by the easily-explained bursting apart of the two sides of the ancient Egyptian figure. Coincidence is a factor in life not always sufficiently considered; and the events I have related can be explained in a perfectly natural manner, if one be inclined to do so.

8.

The Cat That Walked by Himself

by RUDYARD KIPLING

Rudyard Kipling, born in Bombay in 1865, was educated in England, but returned to India where for almost ten years he worked as a journalist. Eventually he settled in London, and rapidly established himself as a master of the storytelling art. His two *Jungle Books* and the *Just So Stories* are placed among the classic animal stories of all time. It is in the latter that we meet "The Cat That Walked by Himself," and learn that independence has its virtues—but also a price.

Hear and attend and listen; for this befell and be-happened and became and was, O my Best Beloved, when the Tame animals were wild. The Dog was wild, and the Horse was wild, and the Cow was wild, and the Sheep was wild, and the Pig was wild—as wild as wild as could be—and they walked in the Wet Wild Woods by their wild lones. But the wildest of all the wild animals was the Cat. He walked by himself, and all places were alike to him.

Of course the Man was wild too. He was dreadfully wild. He didn't even begin to be tame till he met the Woman, and she told him that she did not like living in his wild ways. She picked out a nice dry Cave, instead of a heap of wet leaves, to lie down in; and she strewed clean sand on the floor; and she lit a nice fire of wood at the back of the Cave; and she hung a dried wild-horse skin, tail down, across the opening of the Cave; and she said, "Wipe your feet, dear, when you come in, and now we'll keep house."

That night, Best Beloved, they ate wild sheep roasted on the hot stones, and flavoured with wild garlic and wild pepper; and wild duck stuffed with wild rice and wild fenugreek and wild coriander; and marrow-bones of wild oxen; and wild cherries, and wild grenadillas. Then the Man went to sleep in front of the fire ever so happy; but the Woman sat up, combing her hair. She took the bone of the shoulder of mutton—the big fat blade-bone—and she looked at the wonderful marks on it, and she threw more wood on the fire, and she made a Magic. She made the First Singing Magic in the world.

Out in the Wet Wild Woods all the wild animals gathered together where they could see the light of the fire a long way off, and they wondered what it meant.

Then Wild Horse stamped with his wild foot and said, "O my Friends and O my Enemies, why have the Man and the Woman made that great light in that great Cave, and what harm will it do us?"

Wild Dog lifted up his wild nose and smelled the smell of roast mutton, and said, "I will go up and see and look, and say; for I think it is good. Cat, come with me."

"Nenni!" said the Cat. "I am the Cat who walks by himself, and all places are alike to me. I will not come."

"Then we can never be friends again," said Wild Dog, and he trotted off to the Cave. But when he had gone a little way the Cat said to himself, "All places are alike to me. Why should I not go too and see and look and come away at my own liking." So he slipped after Wild Dog softly, very softly, and hid himself where he could hear everything.

When Wild Dog reached the mouth of the Cave he lifted up the dried horse-skin with his nose and sniffed the beautiful smell of the roast mutton, and the Woman, looking at the blade-bone, heard him, and laughed, and said, "Here comes the first. Wild Thing out of the Wild Woods, what do you want?"

Wild Dog said, "O my Enemy and Wife of my Enemy, what is this that smells so good in the Wild Woods?"

Then the Woman picked up a roasted mutton-bone and threw it to Wild Dog, and said, "Wild Thing out of the Wild Woods, taste and try." Wild Dog gnawed the bone, and it was more delicious than anything he had ever tasted, and he said, "O my Enemy and Wife of my Enemy, give me another."

The Woman said, "Wild Thing out of the Wild Woods, help my Man to hunt through the day and guard this Cave at night, and I will give you as many roast bones as you need."

"Ah!" said the Cat, listening. "This is a very wise Woman, but she is not so wise as I am."

Wild Dog crawled into the Cave and laid his head on the Woman's lap, and said, "O my Friend and Wife of my Friend, I will help your Man to hunt through the day, and at night I will guard your Cave."

"Ah!" said the Cat, listening. "That is a very foolish Dog." And he went back through the Wet Wild Woods waving his wild tail, and walking by his wild lone. But he never told anybody.

When the Man waked up he said, "What is Wild Dog doing here?" And the Woman said, "His name is not Wild Dog any more, but the First Friend, because he will be our friend for always and always and always. Take him with you when you go hunting."

Next night the Woman cut great green armfuls of fresh grass from the water-meadows, and dried it before the fire, so that it smelt like new-mown hay, and she sat at the mouth of the Cave and plaited a halter out of horse-hide, and she looked at the shoulder of mutton-bone—at the big broad blade-bone—and she made a Magic. She made the Second Singing Magic in the world.

Out in the Wild Woods all the wild animals wondered what had happened to Wild Dog, and at last Wild Horse stamped with his foot and said, "I will go and see and say why Wild Dog has not returned. Cat, come with me."

"Nenni!" said the Cat. "I am the Cat who walks by himself, and all places are alike to me. I will not come." But all the same he followed Wild Horse softly, very softly, and hid himself where he could hear everything.

When the Woman heard Wild Horse tripping and stumbling on his long mane, she laughed and said, "Here comes the second. Wild Thing out of the Wild Woods, what do you want?"

Wild Horse said, "O my Enemy and Wife of my Enemy, where is Wild Dog?"

The Woman laughed, and picked up the blade-bone and looked at it, and said, "Wild Thing out of the Wild Woods, you did not come here for Wild Dog, but for the sake of this good grass."

And Wild Horse, tripping and stumbling on his long mane, said, "That is true, give it me to eat."

The Woman said, "Wild Thing out of the Wild Woods,

bend your wild head and wear what I give you, and you shall eat the wonderful grass three times a day."

"Ah," said the Cat, listening, "this is a clever Woman, but she is not so clever as I am."

Wild Horse bent his wild head, and the Woman slipped the plaited hide halter over it, and Wild Horse breathed on the Woman's feet and said, "O my Mistress, and Wife of my Master, I will be your servant for the sake of the wonderful grass."

"Ah," said the Cat, listening. "That is a very foolish Horse." And he went back through the Wet Wild Woods, waving his wild tail and walking by his wild lone. But he never told anybody.

When the Man and the Dog came back from hunting, the Man said, "What is Wild Horse doing here?" And the Woman said, "His name is not Wild Horse any more, but the First Servant, because he will carry us from place to place for always and always and always. Ride on his back when you go hunting."

Next day, holding her wild head high that her wild horns should not catch in the wild trees, Wild Cow came up to the Cave, and the Cat followed, and hid himself just the same as before; and everything happened just the same as before; and the Cat said the same things as before, and when Wild Cow had promised to give her milk to the Woman every day in exchange for the wonderful grass, the Cat went back through the Wet Wild Woods waving his wild tail and walking by his wild lone, just the same as before. But he never told anybody. And when the Man and the Horse and the Dog came home from hunting and asked the same questions same as before, the Woman said, "Her name is not Wild Cow any more, but the Giver of Good Food. She will give us the warm white milk for always and always and always, and I will take care of her while you and the First Friend and the First Servant go hunting."

Next day the Cat waited to see if any other Wild Thing would go up to the Cave, but no one moved in the Wet Wild Woods, so the Cat walked there by himself; and he saw the Woman milking the Cow, and he saw the light of the fire in the Cave, and he smelt the smell of the warm white milk.

Cat said, "O my Enemy, and Wife of my Enemy, where did Wild Cow go?"

The Woman laughed and said, "Wild Thing out of the Wild Woods, go back to the Woods again, for I have braided up my hair, and I have put away the magic blade-bone, and we have no more need of either friends or servants in our Cave."

Cat said, "I'm not a friend, and I'm not a servant. I am the Cat who walks by himself, and I wish to come into your cave."

Woman said, "Then why did you not come with First Friend on the first night?"

Cat grew very angry and said, "Has Wild Dog told tales of me?"

Then the Woman laughed and said, "You are the Cat who walks by himself, and all places are alike to you. You are neither a friend nor a servant. You have said it yourself. Go away and walk by yourself in all places alike."

Then Cat pretended to be sorry and said, "Must I never come into the Cave? Must I never sit by the warm fire? Must I never drink the warm white milk? You are very wise and very beautiful. You should not be cruel even to a Cat."

Woman said, "I knew I was wise, but I did not know I was beautiful. So I will bargain with you. If ever I say one word in your praise you may come into the Cave."

"And if you say two words in my praise?" said the Cat.

"I never shall," said the Woman, "but if I say two words in your praise, you may sit by the fire in the Cave."

"And if you say three words?" said the Cat.

"I never shall," said the Woman, "but if I say three words in your praise, you may drink the warm white milk three times a day for always and always and always."

The the Cat arched his back and said, "Now let the Curtain at the mouth of the Cave, and the Fire at the back of the Cave, and the Milk-pots that stand beside the Fire, remember what my Enemy and the Wife of my Enemy has said." And he went away through the Wet Wild Woods waving his wild tail and walking by his wild lone.

That night when the Man and the Horse and the Dog came home from hunting, the Woman did not tell them of the bargain that she had made with the Cat, because she was afraid that they might not like it.

Cat went far and far away and hid himself in the Wet Wild Woods by his wild lone for a long time till the Woman forgot all about him. Only the Bat—the little upside-down Bat—that hung inside the Cave, knew where Cat hid; and every evening Bat would fly to Cat with news of what was happening.

One evening Bat said, "There is a Baby in the Cave. He is new and pink and fat and small, and the Woman is very fond of him."

"Ah," said the Cat, listening, "but what is the Baby fond of?"

"He is fond of things that are soft and tickle," said the Bat. "He is fond of warm things to hold in his arms when he goes to sleep. He is fond of being played with. He is fond of all those things."

"Ah," said the Cat, listening, "then my time has come."

Next night Cat walked through the Wet Wild Woods and hid very near the Cave till morning-time, and Man and Dog and Horse went hunting. The Woman was busy cooking that morning, and the Baby cried and interrupted. So she carried him outside the Cave and gave him a handful of pebbles to play with. But still the Baby cried.

Then the Cat put out his paddy paw and patted the Baby on the cheek, and it cooed; and the Cat rubbed against its fat knees and tickled it under its fat chin with his tail. And the Baby laughed; and the Woman heard him and smiled.

Then the Bat—the little upside-down Bat—that hung in the mouth of the Cave said, "O my Hostess and Wife of my Host and Mother of my Host's Son, a Wild Thing from the Wild Woods is most beautifully playing with your Baby."

"A blessing on that Wild Thing whoever he may be," said the Woman, straightening her back, "for I was a busy woman this morning and he has done me a service."

That very minute and second, Best Beloved, the dried horse-skin Curtain that was stretched tail-down at the mouth of the Cave fell down—*woosh!*—because it remembered the bargain she had made with the Cat, and when the Woman went to pick it up—lo and behold!—the Cat was sitting quite comfy inside the Cave.

"O my Enemy and Wife of my Enemy and Mother of my Enemy," said the Cat, "it is I; for you have spoken a word in my praise, and now I can sit within the Cave for always and always and always. But still I am the Cat who walks by himself, and all places are alike to me."

The Woman was very angry, and shut her lips tight and took up her spinning-wheel and began to spin.

But the Baby cried because the Cat had gone away, and the
Woman could not hush it, for it struggled and kicked and grew
black in the face.

"O my Enemy and Wife of my Enemy and Mother of my
Enemy," said the Cat, "take a strand of the wire that you are
spinning and tie it to your spinning-whorl and drag it along
the floor, and I will show you a magic that shall make your
Baby laugh as loudly as he is now crying."

"I will do so," said the Woman, "because I am at my wit's
end; but I will not thank you for it."

She tied the thread to the little clay spindle-whorl and
drew it across the floor, and the Cat ran after it and patted
it with his paws and rolled head over heels, and tossed it
backward over his shoulder and chased it between his hind
legs and pretended to lose it, and pounced down upon it
again, till the Baby laughed as loudly as it had been crying,
and scrambled after the Cat and frolicked all over the Cave
till it grew tired and settled down to sleep with the Cat in its
arms.

"Now," said the Cat, "I will sing the Baby a song that
shall keep him asleep for an hour." And he began to purr,
loud and low, low and loud, till the Baby fell fast asleep. The
woman smiled as she looked down upon the two of them and
said, "That was wonderfully done. No question but you
are very clever, O Cat."

That very minute and second, Best Beloved, the smoke of
the fire at the back of the Cave came down in clouds from the
roof—*puff!*—because it remembered the bargain she had
made with the Cat, and when it had cleared away—lo, and
behold!—the Cat was sitting quite comfy close to the fire.

"O my Enemy and Wife of my Enemy and Mother of my
Enemy," said the Cat, "it is I; for you have spoken a second

word in my praise, and now I can sit by the warm fire at the back of the Cave for always and always and always. But still I am the Cat who walks by himself, and all places are alike to me."

Then the Woman was very, very angry, and let down her hair and put more wood on the fire, and brought out the broad blade-bone of the shoulder of mutton and began to make a Magic that should prevent her from saying a third word in praise of the Cat. It was not a Singing Magic, Best Beloved, it was a Still Magic; and by and by the Cave grew so still that a little wee-wee mouse crept out of a corner and ran across the floor.

"O my Enemy and Wife of my Enemy and Mother of my Enemy," said the Cat, "is that little mouse part of your magic?"

"Ouh! Chee! No indeed!" said the Woman, and she dropped the blade-bone and jumped upon the footstool in front of the fire and braided up her hair very quick for fear that the mouse should run up it.

"Ah," said the Cat, watching, "then the mouse will do me no harm if I eat it?"

"No," said the Woman, braiding up her hair, "eat it quickly and I will ever be grateful to you."

Cat made one jump and caught the little mouse, and the Woman said, "A hundred thanks. Even the First Friend is not quick enough to catch little mice as you have done. You must be very wise."

That very moment and second, O Best Beloved, the Milk-pot that stood by the fire cracked in two pieces—*ffft*— because it remembered the bargain she had made with the Cat, and when the Woman jumped down from the footstool —lo and behold!—the Cat was lapping up the warm white milk that lay in one of the broken pieces.

"O my Enemy and Wife of my Enemy and Mother of my Enemy," said the Cat, "it is I; for you have spoken three words in my praise, and now I can drink the warm white milk three times a day for always and always. But *still* I am the Cat who walks by himself, and all places are alike to me."

Then the Woman laughed and set the Cat a bowl of the warm white milk and said, "O Cat, you are as clever as a man, but remember that your bargain was not made with the Man or the Dog, and I do not know what they will do when they come home."

"What is that to me?" said the Cat. "If I have my place in the Cave by the fire and my warm white milk three times a day I do not care what the Man or the Dog can do."

That evening when the Man and the Dog came into the Cave, the Woman told them all the story of the bargain while the Cat sat by the fire and smiled. Then the Man said, "Yes, but he has not made a bargain with *me* or with all proper Men after me." Then he took off his two leather boots and he took up his little stone axe (that makes three) and he fetched a piece of wood and a hatchet (that is five altogether), and he set them out in a row and he said, "Now we will make *our* bargain. If you do not catch mice when you are in the Cave for always and always and always, I will throw these five things at you whenever I see you, and so shall all proper Men do after me."

"Ah," said the Woman, listening, "this is a very clever Cat, but he is not so clever as my Man."

The Cat counted the five things (and they looked very knobby) and he said, "I will catch mice when I am in the Cave for always and always and always; but *still* I am the Cat who walks by himself, and all places are alike to me."

"Not when I am near," said the Man. "If you had not said that last I would have put all these things away for always and always and always; but I am now going to throw my two boots and my little stone axe (that makes three) at you whenever I meet you. And so shall all proper Men do after me!"

Then the Dog said, "Wait a minute. He has not made a bargain with *me* or with all proper Dogs after me." And he showed his teeth and said, "If you are not kind to the Baby while I am in the Cave for always and always and always, I will hunt you till I catch you, and when I catch you I will bite you. And so shall all proper Dogs do after me."

"Ah," said the Woman, listening, "this is a very clever Cat, but he is not so clever as the Dog."

Cat counted the Dog's teeth (and they looked very pointed) and he said, "I will be kind to the Baby while I am in the Cave, as long as he does not pull my tail too hard, for always and always and always. But *still* I am the Cat that walks by himself, and all places are alike to me."

"Not when I am near," said the Dog. "If you had not said that last I would have shut my mouth for always and always and always; but *now* I am going to hunt you up a tree whenever I meet you. And so shall all proper Dogs do after me."

Then the Man threw his two boots and his little stone axe (that makes three) at the Cat, and the Cat ran out of the Cave and the Dog chased him up a tree; and from that day to this, Best Beloved, three proper Men out of five will always throw things at a Cat whenever they meet him, and all the proper Dogs will chase him up a tree. But the Cat keeps his side of the bargain too. He will kill mice and he will be kind to Babies when he is in the house, just as long as they do not pull his tail too hard. But when he has done that, and between times, and when the moon gets up and night comes, he is the Cat that walks by himself, and all places are alike to him.

Then he goes out to the Wet Wild Woods or up the Wet Wild Trees or on the Wet Wild Roofs, waving his wild tail and walking by his wild lone.

9.

The Old Cat and the Young Mouse

by JEAN DE LA FONTAINE

A young Mouse, small and innocent,
Implored an old Cat's clemency:
"Raminagrobis, let me live!
Your royal mercy, monarch, give!
A Mouse so little, sir, as I
A tiny meal can ill supply.
How could I starve a family?
Host, hostess, only look at me.
I fatten on a grain of wheat,—
A mite my dinner makes complete;
I'm thin, too, now,—just wait a bit,
And for your children I'll be fit."
Thus spoke the little Mouse, aggrieved;
The old Cat answered: "You're deceived.
Go, tell the deaf and dumb,—not me,
Cats never pardon, so you'll see.
The law condemns, and you must die;
Descend, and tell the Fates that I
Have stopped your preaching, and be sure
My children's meals will be no fewer."
He kept his word; and to my fable
I add a moral, as I'm able:
Youth hopes to win all by address;
But age is ever pitiless.

10.

A Fine Place for the Cat

by MARGARET BONHAM

Margaret Bonham shares with us a very British, very amusing tale of a mail-order cat who turns out to be not quite what her mistress expected—a cat with "fur as flat as a skinned rabbit and a face as pointed as a piece of cheese and eyes as blue as china and squinting inwards towards its nose." Tulan, not convinced at all by accusations that she is "some kind of monkey," proceeds to become great friends with the fish-man—and from there it's clear sailing.

Twice a week the green van came to the village; on the same two days Mrs. Miller was up at half-past eight and leaning out of the sitting-room window. Her lank hair and her dirty and faded casement curtains blew about in the wind, and out of the sitting-room window she leaned to watch the cats; for Mrs. Miller, though she was indeed a fat slut and had no beauty and few virtues, felt strongly enough about cats to get out of her bed an hour or more early two days a week winter and summer; and no other passion she was capable of had anything but the opposite effect.

Mrs. Miller did not often or consciously look at the fish-man himself, and nor did any of the women who came out through their swinging gates with a dish in their hands and a leather purse. Mrs. Miller watched the cats from her window, and the women, standing one or two at a time in the half-secure screen of the van's open doors, looked no higher than his hands weighing, than the herrings and mackerel, the scales and the lifting from the tray to their dish; more than capable he was of slipping a little herring from clean under their noses down to Mrs. Rhys's Tab who yelled for it beside his boots. If his attention were distracted for a moment the women would shoo and scuff at Mrs. Rhys's Tab with their squashed slippers, and Mrs. Rhys's Tab would curl round to the other side of the fish-man's boots; and Mrs. Miller would put out her tongue at the women from her window.

Neither Mrs. Miller nor any of the women who came out to buy herrings and mackerel could have told you anything about the fish-man, except: he likes cats; medium tall he is, and thin; he wears a brown suit and a blue apron, his hair is drab, or greyish; cats is it with him, all the time. The village, except for Mrs. Miller, thought him mad. Mad in this way is anyone who gives to cats what he might sell to women.

On Tuesdays and Fridays when the green van came to the village the tom cat from the Seven Stars waited on the stone pillar at the end of the bridge. Down from the driving-seat climbed the fish man to open the doors at the back, and the Seven Stars' cat, already at his feet with its wide cheeks puffed wider, put one paw on his leg and opened its triangular mouth for the consummation of whiting that the fish-man wedged into it, head and tail drooping on either side. The whiting and the Seven Stars' cat went off like a rocket into the yard of the inn; the fish-man, disinterested, weighed out plaice for the landlord. Beyond Mrs. Miller's cottage, down the street, all the other cats waited at their gates.

All the other cats waited for the fish-man and their whiting, in the early morning sun, and the smell of breakfast and bees-wax and the all-important smell of fish; in the cottages the children sat moving their mouths ringed with milk, and from her window Mrs. Miller watched the fish-man drive past her from the Seven Stars to the other cottages, to the church gates; from the church gates back down the street, to stop last of all at her door. Though she did not like fish she ate it for dinner on Tuesdays and Fridays, in her parlour which was dirty and faded like the green casement curtains and had a dark circle on the buff wallpaper where she leaned back when she had finished, with her greasy head against the wall, a Woodbine in the corner of her mouth and her own cat Henry on her knees hooking fish-bones off the plate and chewing them one-sided on her stained cotton overall. He was an old cat; age after the fashion of age had taken away his good shape and by nature he was not intelligent; he did not even to Mrs. Miller's eyes seem impressive, seem the sort of cat one would be proud to see sitting outside the gate waiting for the fish-man, but she was fond of him. The fish-man, looking at Henry teetering away behind a whiting, would say with an air of melancholy: "Indeed it seems wrong for a cat to be old, Mrs. Miller." True, Mrs. Miller thought; but she said: "Well, fond of them you get, like."

In the winter Henry died. Mrs. Miller grieved over him and refused the offer of a bastard kitten from the Seven Stars; but the fish-man's visits became meaningless talking of other people's cats and in time she began to think about getting another of her own. A great deal she thought about it, and saw herself with a beautiful and impressive cat like none of her neighbours', like no other cat in the village. The fish-man leaned on her gate in the snow and said: "When will there be another Henry, now, Mrs. Miller?" "Maybe soon, now," said Mrs. Miller, looking remotely up at the dark trees laced white against the dark sky, behind his head. She took her two herrings on a plate and went flapping and crackling in her broken slippers up the snowy path and into her parlour to light the fire. She put the herrings on the rug beside her and sat on her heels pulling out from behind the coal-scuttle the crumpled paper in which Friday's cod had been wrapped. But when it was in the grate the word CATS looked at her between the bars and she pulled it out again and smoothed it on her knee, the front page of *The Times*. Feeling in her overall pocket for a bent cigarette, she read:

Pedigree female Siamese kitten for sale, 4
months; house-trained, sings, 3½ gns., carriage paid.
Letchley, Elm House, Hastock, Shrops.

Mrs. Miller, with an unlit Woodbine in the corner of her mouth, sat and stared at the empty grate, seeing in its crusted depths a firm picture of her front path and an elegant cat treading it like a heraldic creature and a tail like a dark gold ostrich plume waving against the snow. Mrs. Miller had never seen a Siamese cat in her life. She got up from the hearthrug, leaving the herrings, and went to look for her wicked husband's typewriter, because she knew she had not the sort of handwriting in which to order a pedigree Siamese cat. It was a short letter and took her most of the morning. When it was finished she put a coat on top of her overall and went out and took some money from her post office account and added some more from the housekeeping and bought postal orders for three and a half guineas. Then she stuck a stamp on the letter and went back and lit the fire.

"Well now, where is the new Henry, Mrs. Miller?" said the fish-man on Friday, leaning on the white-edged gate; and Mrs. Miller looked up at the trees and said: "Coming any day now. A new sort of cat I'm getting," she said, staring up at the sky closing like a grey oyster-shell over the village; "a valuable cat," she said with a casual folding of her dirty overall round her neck against the cold wind. "There's good news, Mrs. Miller, indeed," said the fish-man, "a Persian cat, is it?"

"No," said Mrs. Miller, "not an old Persian. Something different in the way of a cat it will be; not till it comes will you see what sort of a cat it is." "I hope it comes fast," said the fish-man, "for I can't wait to know." "Like enough by Tuesday," said Mrs. Miller. "It's a she-cat," she said over her shoulder as she flapped away up the path.

The letter came saying when the elegant new cat would arrive at the station. There were some furtive feelings in Mrs. Miller that she must look impressive for such a cat's first view of her, and she put on her best blue costume and pearl earrings and the coat with a piece of fur, and combed her hair round her fingers and walked a mile through the snow to the station in black shoes with high heels. She sat half an hour in the waiting-room, for the train was late, but when it came in at last with the single carriage furred with a rim of smoky snow she shot into the luggage office and leaned against the counter like a lady while Mr. Jones who did everything at the station brought in a bicycle and a wicker basket of hens and a smaller basket like someone's picnic lunch. Mr. Jones put the smaller basket on the counter and it gave out a most appalling howl; a howl in a minor key it was, to make your blood run cold. "God save us," said Mr. Jones, stepping back into the bicycle, "what is in there, Mrs. Miller?" "A cat, it is," said Mrs. Miller uncertainly, and leaned forward to point out the label saying VALUABLE CAT tied to the handle. "Indeed that is no cat," said Mr. Jones, "cats mew. Let us have a look, now," he said, and took hold of the strap with caution; but Mrs. Miller, hypnotized by the howl, said quickly: "No, Mr. Jones, I will be taking it home with me now. What would we do if it got out?" Mr. Jones shook his head and said: "You should not be opening it at home with no man in the house; indeed, Mrs. Miller, I should come and stand over it with the poker." "No poker will I have waved over my pedigree cat, Mr. Jones," said Mrs. Miller, recovering her aplomb, "and a cat it is for sure; I bought it out of the paper; it howls with fright from your old train." And she picked up the basket firmly and went out to the snowy road; by the time she got home to the cottage she was reconciled to such strangeness in a cat's voice and could not without difficulty wait to open the basket and see this elegant exotic creature that was to have dark-gold feathery fur and a tail like an ostrich plume.

So she put the basket on the parlour table before even she had taken off her coat, and undid the label and the strap and the catch and threw back the lid; and then reeling towards the fireplace she went with a melodramatic gesture like someone in a play and cried: "God help us!" knowing she had been sold for a fool and palmed off with some kind of monkey. Away went Mrs. Miller's visions of long gold fur and golden plumes; such a sense of embarrassment she had now, thinking of what the fish-man would say, and the neighbours, and whether the creature would spring on her and howl, for she could see only the top half looking out of the basket. A creature it was for sure and not a cat, thought Mrs. Miller; what cat has fur as flat as a skinned rabbit and a face as pointed as a piece of cheese and eyes as blue as china and squinting inwards to its nose? And what cat was called not Henry or Tab or Smut, but Tulan Caprian of Hastock? Mrs. Miller spelt it out on the label. Disbelievingly

she went on staring, and so did Tulan; disbelievingly she
said "Puss . . .?" and went back another step when Tulan
climbed out of the basket on to the table; truly Mrs. Miller
would not have been surprised to see four green paws and a
red tail with a fork on the end, and was hardly less taken
aback by these thin legs like a Victorian dancer's in dark
stockings and a tail no thicker it seemed to Mrs. Miller (who
had not even now entirely given up thoughts of ostrich
plumes) than a piece of tarred string. "Well, God save us,
delirious I must be," she said to herself, and put the kettle
on the fire with one eye on Tulan. Tulan sat on the table with
that tail curled round those feet, and presently gave a tenta-
tive amiable howl. Mrs. Miller, jumping at the tenor key,
quickly took a plate of fish out of the cupboard and edged
it on to the brown plush cloth. "Well," she said under her
breath, "one queer-looking monster you are and no mistake." She backed away to the kitchen and made herself a
cup of tea, which was not really what she wanted, but the
Seven Stars was shut.

Alone in the parlour, in a shell of lamplight and firelight,
away from the dark and snow outside, they spent the evening, Tulan confidently and Mrs. Miller with a shocked dis-
trust. Every time she looked at the azure squint, the dark thin
legs, the dark-brown tail like a monkey's and the flat short
fur the colour of pale oatmeal with a glitter like the sun on
snow, she thought about what the neighbours would say and
above all the fish-man tomorrow morning. Tulan sat in front
of the fire with her dark pointed ears pricked up, turning the
nearer one towards Mrs. Miller when she sighed or muttered,
as if in politeness to lose no word of what she said. This was
unnerving; Mrs. Miller fell silent and smoked a chain of
bewildered cigarettes. At half-past nine she made herself an-

other cup of tea, and Tulan for the first time jumped into her lap, curling dark feet under a pale swansdown breast, and purring. At half-past ten she could not be left alone and wild in the kitchen or the parlour for the night. She slept on Mrs. Miller's bed.

Because of the fish-man the alarm clock was set for a quarter-past eight. Mrs. Miller woke to see Tulan square in her line of vision and six inches from her eyes. She recoiled and got out of bed. At once she thought of the fish-man and wished she were safe in solitude, his visit past; but she said to herself: "I will have to get it over, and a nuisance it will be; indeed, he is sure to laugh at the creature; but I will get it over and out of the way." She put on her clothes and her messy faded overall, and went down with Tulan to the kitchen.

When the fire was lit she slopped into the parlour and looked out of the window. There the green van stood outside the Seven Stars, and the black tom cat (a cat to reassure you after the what-you-will chewing the table-cloth fringe behind your back) was galloping off with his whiting between the red and snowy pillars of the yard entrance. All down the

street the green van went, stopping and selling fish to the
women who came out with white dishes and strawberry noses
into the cold, stopping and giving fish to the fine ordinary
cats that mewed as cats should and rubbed their properly furred
and covered flanks against the fish-man's boots; down the
street it went to the church gates, watched with growing mis-
giving by Mrs. Miller from behind her stained and faded green
curtains, turned round, and drove back to her cottage. Mrs.
Miller looked despairingly at Tulan, picked up the enamel dish
and went out of the blistered door.

"Well, Mrs. Miller, now," said the fish-man with his hand
on the gate, "will the grand new cat be here yet?"

Mrs. Miller looked up at the trees. "Well," she said re-
pressively, "arrived it has for sure; but indeed it's not the
sort of cat I expected. It's a great wonder to me," she said
with a rush, preparing him for the worst, "that it passes for a
cat at all."

"Very sad that is, Mrs. Miller, now, if it's not what you
hoped," said the fish-man, "but perhaps it's only she will not
be feeling herself after the journey."

"Oh, no," said Mrs. Miller on a round note, thinking of
the parlour table-cloth, "she is feeling herself all right; her
looks it is that are not like a proper cat's at all." She tapped
her fingers on the enamel dish and stared up at the trees in
silence, but the fish-man was looking over her shoulder at the
door. He looked past her at the cottage and the open door,
and cried with such an air of surprise that she was startled.
"Why, Mrs. Miller," he cried, "why, she's a beauty!" Mrs.
Miller turned round and saw Tulan, seeming very small,
treading with her dark-legged dancer's step up the snowy
path, with her dark ears pointed to the breath of fish, her
dark thin tail like a question mark up from the pale thin

line of her back; Mrs. Miller looked at her and saw with a shock that she was a beauty indeed. Now all the other cats seemed gross and without shape. But she said nothing, only stared at Tulan and tapped her fingers on the enamel dish; and Tulan trod up to the fish-man and gave her urgent howl.

The fish-man was enchanted; he took her up in his arms and said: "Why, Mrs. Miller, this is the greatest beauty of a cat I've seen in a lifetime, for sure. God save us, Mrs. Miller," he said, "were you telling me you were disappointed in a cat like this? What sort of cat is it called, now?" "It's a Siamese cat," said Mrs. Miller, caught out in the wrong opinion and a little cross, "and a big cat I thought it would be with a great tail like feathers." "So help me," said the fish-man, "will you look at the blue eyes? What would you want with a lot of fur and no bones? Losing her to me you will be, Mrs. Miller, if she's not the cat you wanted."

"Well, I do want her," said Mrs. Miller quickly; "it's getting used to her is a matter of time." She looked at Tulan and then at the fish-man, and in a moment she laughed; meeting the fish-man's eyes over Tulan's head like two people in a film over the head of a reconciling child, for the first time Mrs. Miller impaled him with a direct stare and saw that his eyes were as blue as the cat's; and for his part the fish-man thought the cat's eyes were not more blue than hers. Tulan breathed fish over his shoulder, and howled. "Well, Mrs. Miller," he said, and turned to the van, "we will see what the beautiful cat would like." He picked up a whiting by its tail and held it over Tulan who embraced it like a monkey, and hanging on by claws and teeth was lowered through the air to the ground. Mrs. Miller and the fish-man stood in the snow and watched the whiting disappear faster than you could believe.

With Tulan there was no doubt the fish-man was a success. "What does your husband say to such a cat, now?" he said suddenly. Mrs. Miller opened her eyes as startled as if Tulan had asked instead: she had not believed him capable of talking about anything but cats and fish, and the weather. "That I couldn't tell you," she said, "for he's not here." "In the Forces he would be, I expect," said the fish-man; and Mrs. Miller said: "Very likely, indeed, if they are not too particular; three years it is since he set eyes on me and I would be sorry if I saw him again." "That's a sad thing for you, Mrs. Miller," said the fish-man, "and grieved I am to hear it, but we all make mistakes." Mrs. Miller looked at the high trees, and after a pause she said: "Well, I will be going in now." "Well, you will take another little fish for the beautiful cat," said the fish-man, leaning over Tulan in passionate admiration and slapping a whiting as large as a dogfish on to Mrs. Miller's enamel dish, "and on Friday I will be seeing the cat again. There is something to look forward to, Mrs. Miller," he said, standing with his elbow on the gate, watching both of them go up the path, Mrs. Miller scrunching and scuffing in her broken slippers and Tulan prancing behind howling and flipping up her back legs. Both he and Mrs. Miller, with one mind, had forgotten the two herrings that Mrs. Miller had come out to buy for her dinner.

Having accepted Tulan, Mrs. Miller found that it meant what might almost be called hard work. Tulan's passion was inevitably for the front line. She could not be forgotten for hours at a time and satisfied with a stroke and a plate of fish; she would be talked to incessantly, and carried her side of the conversation with a positive conviction; she would not be left alone. Mrs. Miller found herself playing exacting games on the stairs, playing bending three feet from the ground to be patted on both temples, playing with balls of paper for Tulan to fly somersaulting round the room without touching the floor. Soon, since Tulan howled when she was left, Mrs. Miller began to take her out shopping in the village, held in a fold of her coat. The village people, disapproving, called her "Mrs. Miller's monkey." Now Tulan slept in bed with her head against Mrs. Miller's neck on the pillow, and Mrs. Miller put on extra face cream for Tulan to lick off. She was an unsentimental, affectionate slut of a creature and Tulan's company suited her down to the ground; the next best thing she was to the right man, and even then less trouble.

Longer and longer the fish-man stayed leaning over the gate on Tuesdays and Fridays, talking to both of them; his gifts to Tulan inflated so in size that indeed Mrs. Miller would not have been surprised to see him drag a shark out of his van any moment. "I am thinking I will have to have a cat like this for myself, Mrs. Miller," he said, "for seeing her twice a week is not enough." Mrs. Miller leaned her elbow on the rotting gatepost and looked over his head. "What would your wife think of that?" she said, and the fish-man watched Tulan with a whiting as big as herself and said: "There is no wife in my house and never has been." "Then who looks after you?" said Mrs. Miller, and he said: "Why for sure, I look after myself. There is no worry for me in not having things as they should be," he said, "for a cat or two and plenty to eat and a good fire is enough." "That's right indeed," said Mrs. Miller, stooping to run her finger between Tulan's ears. She looked up at him with her greasy hair falling in her eyes and smirked to show her white teeth. "Enough for anyone, for sure," she said.

The snow melted and Tulan grew a shade larger and sometimes the fish-man stayed talking for an hour or more;

when Tulan was too full of fish to howl for more she would sit on his shoulder and wash her Oriental face, and Mrs. Miller would prop herself against the still-rotting gatepost which creaked on and off under her considerable weight, and they would talk cats till their throats were dry. This was something for the village to gossip about under its breath in the shops, how long the green van stayed outside the cottage; but never more than a yard from it went Mrs. Miller and the fish-man, so there was no surmise of absence to add interest, and for her part Mrs. Miller was secure in herself and cared not a straw what was said. Now when she looked up over the fish-man's head at the tall line of trees on the hill they were dark with the red colour of advancing spring. "This sort of weather I would like to be going on holiday," she said to the fish-man; and the fish-man said quickly, as if he had been waiting: "Would you like a little drive in the van, now?"

Mrs. Miller went on staring at the trees in silence; at last she said: "Indeed, that would be a nice change; where is it you will be going from here?" "Pleased I would be to take you anywhere you want," said the fish-man, "but if you would like it we could take Tulan to see my cats. Not a very good house, mine is, but she would be welcome." "That would be a change for Tulan too," said Mrs. Miller, looking at him carefully and seeming pleased with what she saw. She went flapping up the damp path into the kitchen, and put on her coat, and took eighteen and nine-pence out of the teapot on the shelf and her Post Office Savings book from the chaos behind the mangle, and snapped them into a dirty handbag, and went out and shut the door behind her. The fish-man leaned on the gate, and Tulan sat on his shoulder beginning to howl for more whiting, for the first lot was an hour past and she had room again. "She will not have been in a motor before, I expect," said the fish-man, and swung her down on to his arm. "Well there, is everything ready, then?" he said, looking at Mrs. Miller; and Mrs. Miller said: "For sure everything is ready, now," and shut the gate with a bang that broke the post. Mrs. Miller knew, and the fish-man knew, that she would not come back to the cottage again except to settle her affairs; but they said nothing.

"There is a fine place for the beautiful cat," said the fish-man, and he put the speechless Tulan into the back of the van with all the sprats and whiting and herrings, and shut the doors.

"A fine place indeed," said Mrs. Miller, and sitting beside him in the front, on a torn fishy cushion, she watched Tulan through the little window while they drove past the Seven Stars and out of the village.

11.

Good and Bad Kittens

by OLIVER HERFORD

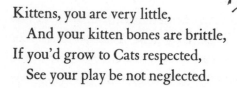

Kittens, you are very little,
  And your kitten bones are brittle,
If you'd grow to Cats respected,
  See your play be not neglected.

Smite the Sudden Spool, and spring
  Upon the Swift Elusive String;
Thus you learn to catch the wary
  Mister Mouse, or Miss Canary.

That is how, in Foreign Places,
  Fluffy Cubs with Kitten faces,
Where the mango waves sedately,
  Grow to Lions large and stately.

But the Kittencats who snatch
  Rudely for their food, or scratch,
Grow to Tomcats gaunt and gory,
  Theirs is quite another story.

Cats like these are put away
  By the dread S. P. C. A.,
Or to trusting Aunts and Sisters
  Sold as Sable Muffs and Wristers.

12.

Puss in Boots

by CHARLES PERRAULT

Charles Perrault, a Frenchman of the seventeenth century, is best known for his authorship of the traditional *Tales from Mother Goose*. To this dedicated storyteller we owe thanks for many of the nursery rhymes which were chanted to us as young children, as well as for much of the rich heritage of fairy tales with which we grew up. In "Puss in Boots," otherwise known as "The Master Cat," we meet another clever cat who, starting only with a pair of boots and an active imagination, earns honor, riches, and happiness for himself and his master.

THERE was a miller who left no more estate to the three sons he had than his mill, his donkey and his cat. The division was soon made. Neither scrivener nor attorney was sent for; they would soon have eaten up all the poor patrimony. The eldest had the mill, the second the donkey, and the youngest nothing but the cat. The poor young fellow was quite comfortless at having so poor a lot.

"My brothers," said he, "may get their living handsomely enough by joining their stocks together. But for my part, when I have eaten my cat, and made me a muff of his skin, I must die of hunger."

The cat, who heard all this, said to him with a grave and serious air, "Do not thus afflict yourself, my good master. You need only give me a bag, and have a pair of boots made for

me that I may scamper through the brambles. You shall see you have not so bad a portion with me as you imagine."

The cat's master had often seen him play a great many cunning tricks to catch rats and mice; he used to hide himself in the meal, and make as if he were dead; so he did not altogether despair. When the cat had what he asked for, he booted himself very gallantly, and putting his bag about his neck, he held the strings of it in his two forepaws and went into a warren where there was a great abundance of rabbits. He put bran and lettuce into his bag and, stretching out at length as if dead, he waited for some young rabbits, not yet acquainted with the deceits of the world, to come and rummage for what he had put into his bag.

Scarce had he lain down but he had what he wanted: a rash and foolish young rabbit jumped into his bag. Monsieur Puss, immediately drawing close the strings, killed him without pity. Proud of his prey, he went with it to the palace, and asked to speak with his majesty. He was shown into the king's apartment and, making a low reverence, said to him:

"I have brought you, sir, a rabbit from the warren, which my noble lord, the Marquis of Carabas"—for that was the title Puss was pleased to give his master—"has commanded me to present to Your Majesty from him."

"Tell your master," said the king, "that I thank him, and that he gives me a great deal of pleasure."

Another time the cat hid himself among some standing corn, holding his bag open. When a brace of partridges ran into it, he drew the strings and so caught them both. He made a present of these to the king as he had the rabbit. The king, in like manner, received the partridges with great pleasure, and ordered some money to be given to him.

The cat continued thus for two or three months to carry to his majesty, from time to time, game of his master's taking. One day in particular, when he knew for certain that the king was to take the air along the riverside with his daughter, the most beautiful princess in the world, he said to his master:

"If you will follow my advice your fortune is made. You have nothing to do but wash yourself in the river, where I shall show you, and leave the rest to me."

The Marquis of Carabas did what the cat advised him to do, without knowing why or wherefore. While he was washing, the king passed by, and the cat began to cry out:

"Help! Help! My Lord Marquis of Carabas is going to be drowned."

At this the king put his head out of the coach window, and finding it was the cat who had so often brought him such good game, he commanded his guards to run immediately to the assistance of his lordship the Marquis of Carabas. While they were drawing him out of the river, the cat came up to the coach and told the king that, while his master was washing, there came by some rogues, who went off with his clothes, though he had cried out, "Thieves! Thieves!" several times, as loud as he could.

This cunning cat had hidden them under a great stone. The king immediately commanded the officers of his ward-

robe to run and fetch one of his best suits for the Marquis of
Carabas.

The fine clothes set off his good mien, for he was well
made and very handsome in his person. The king's daughter
took a secret inclination to him, and the Marquis of Carabas
had no sooner cast two or three respectful and tender glances
upon her than she fell in love with him to distraction. The
king would needs have him come into the coach and take the
air with them. The cat, quite overjoyed to see his project begin
to succeed, marched on before, and meeting with some country-
men, who were mowing a meadow, he said to them:

"Good people, you who are mowing, if you do not tell the
king that the meadow you mow belongs to my Lord Marquis of Carabas, you shall be chopped as small as herbs for
the pot."

The king did not fail to ask the mowers to whom the
meadow belonged.

"To my Lord Marquis of Carabas," they answered altogether, for the cat's threat had made them terribly afraid.

"You see, sir," said the marquis, "this is a meadow which
never fails to yield a plentiful harvest every year."

The Master Cat, who still went on before, met with some
reapers, and said to them, "Good people, you who are reap-
ing, if you do not tell the king that all this corn belongs to
the Marquis of Carabas you shall be chopped as small as
herbs for the pot."

The king, who passed by a moment after, wished to know
to whom all that corn belonged.

"To my Lord Marquis of Carabas," replied the reapers,
and the king was very well pleased with it, as well as with
the marquis, whom he congratulated thereupon. The Master
Cat, who went always before, said the same words to all he

met, and the king was astonished at the vast estates of the Marquis of Carabas.

Monsieur Puss came at last to a stately castle, the master of which was an ogre, the richest ever known. All the lands which the king had then gone over belonged to this ogre. The cat, who had taken care to inform himself who this ogre was and what he could do, asked to speak with him, saying he could not pass so near his castle without paying his respects to him.

The ogre received him as civilly as an ogre could and made him sit down.

"I have been assured," said the cat, "that you have the gift of being able to change yourself into any sort of creature. You can, for example, transform yourself into a lion or elephant and the like."

"That is true," answered the ogre briskly, "and to convince you, you shall see me now become a lion."

Puss was so badly terrified at the sight of a lion so near him that he immediately got into the rain gutter, not without abundance of trouble and danger, because of his boots. They were of no use walking upon the tiles. A little while after, when Puss saw that the ogre had resumed his natural form, he came down and owned he had been very much frightened.

"I have been moreover informed," said the cat, "but I know not how to believe it, that you have also the power to take on the shape of the smallest animal; for example, to change yourself into a rat or a mouse; but I must own to you I take this to be impossible."

"Impossible!" cried the ogre. "You'll see that presently."

At the same time he changed himself into a mouse and began to run about the floor. Puss no sooner perceived this than he fell upon him and ate him up.

Meanwhile the king, who saw, as he passed, this fine castle of the ogre's, had a mind to go into it. Puss, who heard the noise of his majesty's coach running over the drawbridge, ran out, and said to the king:

"Your Majesty is welcome to this castle of my Lord Marquis of Carabas."

"What, my Lord Marquis!" cried the king. "And does this castle also belong to you? There can be nothing finer than this court and all the stately buildings which surround it. Let us go in, if you please."

The marquis gave his hand to the princess and followed the king, who went first. They passed into a spacious hall, where they found a magnificent collation, which the ogre had prepared for his friends, who were that very day to visit him, but dared not enter, knowing the king was there. His majesty was charmed with the good qualities of the Lord Marquis of Carabas, as was his daughter, and seeing the vast estate he possessed, said to him:

"It will be owing to yourself only, my Lord Marquis, if you are not my son-in-law."

The marquis, making several bows, accepted the honor which his majesty conferred upon him, and forthwith, that very same day, married the princess.

Puss became a great lord, and never ran after mice any more.

13.

The Castle of Carabas

by SYLVIA TOWNSEND WARNER

Sylvia Townsend Warner is an English writer whose poetry, novels, and short stories are much appreciated for their whimsical and satirical fantasy. But she departs from her usual lighthearted approach in "The Castle of Carabas" to tell us an old-fashioned haunted-house tale. We got our first glimpse of this castle and its inhabitants in "Puss in Boots"; now, as we view it in a new light, we can't help but wonder if it's the ghost of Puss that haunts the castle here—or is it a ghost at all?

For five generations the heirs to the marquisate of Carabas had come into the world with a peculiar birth-mark, like the imprint of a cat's paw, and with a horror of cats.

The birth-mark was, under the circumstances, comprehensible; for the castle of Carabas, though situated on one of the healthiest mountains in Navarre, is remote from any society, and thus five marchionesses of Carabas had spent the most sensitive year of married life with little or nothing to look at except the armorial bearings of the marquisate, of which by far the most striking feature is the crest: *a cat rampant, booted and tached proper.*

The horror of cats is less easy to explain; for the Carabas crest records the exploit of the first marquis, who overcame a cat in single combat; but a cat of such gigantic size and hellish cunning and malevolence that the deed was considerably more than it sounds at first hearing.

The cat, in all the grimness of heraldry, dominated the castle. Carved in stone it guarded the park gates and the main doorway, and ranged along the battlements alternately with small cannon was silhouetted against the sky. Engraved on silver its rampings were fixed on every spoon, tureen, and porringer. Carved in wood or modelled in plaster it supported fireplaces, buffets, and beds, and confronted one at each turning of the staircase. It was embroidered on the linen, painted on the coach, carved in half-relief on the backs of the dining-room chairs (which made them very uncomfortable to lean back on), inlaid on floors, painted in windows, embossed on ceilings. It was also a conspicuous motive in the decorative scheme of the chapel.

There was, too, a large and curious oil-painting which was put out as a hatchment at the death of any of the family. It represented the first marquis just before the combat began. Serene and confident, he measures the strength of the animal, which is standing on its hind-legs and menacing him with its paw. In the distance is a mill. The canvas is said to be by Velazquez.

There were, of course, no living cats in or about the establishment. The mice were kept down by specially trained monkeys.

Anything hereditary becomes with course of time creditable, and the Carabas birth-mark, though unbecoming, and the Carabas swooning-fits, though inconvenient, were inseparably part of the family honours. When, in the sixth generation, a son was born there was a quiet satisfaction but no surprise that the cat's paw birth-mark was strongly impressed on his cheek. The boy (he was the only child to survive infancy) was named Ildefonso, after the first marquis, and brought up in the usual manner—that is to say, entirely within the castle boundaries, where no cats could cross his path.

He was a sickly child, and inclined to be intelligent. From his infancy he showed a particular reverence for the family crest, and almost the first word he uttered was *gato*. His father, Don Salvador, used to draw little cats on paper to please him, copying with a shaky hand the heraldic animal, all boots and whiskers, and giving it a tremendous tail that curled like a dragon's and was forked at the tip.

One day Doña Claridad said:

"You know, my dear, that is not in the least like a real cat."

"No?" said the marquis. "I have never seen one."

"What is a real cat?" asked the child.

Doña Claridad gave a little mew.

"*Mon amie*," said the marquis reprovingly, "*pas devant l'enfant*. Now, Ildefonso, we will draw an archbishop."

"No, no! Show me the marquises."

"The marquis, child. Your great-great-great-great-grandfather. Ildefonso el combatidor. The other figure is the wicked cat."

They walked to the end of the long gallery, the sickly child and the grave weakly man, and stood before the canvas.

"Why did he kill the cat?"

"Because it was a wicked cat, my child. A traitor, a Judas."

"What did it do, Father?"

"That story can never be told. It is so terrible that it has to be forgotten."

All over the castle the child went with his question. What

did the cat do? In the stables they told him that it was a wicked cat, and perhaps—who knows?—rode the horses into lather. In the kitchen they said it was probably a thief. In the linen-room they said that it had dirty habits. His tutor, who was also the librarian, said that the cat was an embodiment of evil, and perhaps a symbol of heresy and the Albigenses. Then he told the child about the Albigenses, the Cathari, and the Manichees.

Though the child listened attentively, in the end he walked away hanging his head and saying sorrowfully:

"But they were not real cats, either."

One morning, a little before the child's eighth birthday, Doña Claridad heard a great outcry coming from the courtyard. She opened the shutters and looked down. Below was a circle of men-servants and maid-servants, all screaming and shouting, some wringing their hands, some brandishing brooms, rakes, and horse-whips, some beating on frying-pans, and others clutching their rosaries. Words detached themselves from the hubbub, and rebounded echoing from the castle wall.

"The cat! The monkey! The cat! The cat! The Virgin! The monkey! The devil! The saints! The monkey! The cat!"

In the center of the ring one of the castle monkeys was bounding to and fro, holding something in its front paw. What it held was a kitten.

The uproar increased.

"The cat! The monkey! The monkey! The child! The cat! The Virgin! The smelling-salts! The child! *The child!*"

Bruising her hands on the iron lattice, Doña Claridad saw from her window the child Ildefonso squirm through the crowd and step into the center of the ring, and cuff the monkey. It chattered at him, and he cuffed it again, and it dropped the kitten. One of the gardeners ran forward swinging his spade; but before he could batter the kitten to death Ildefonso had picked it up.

He held it close to his face and gently rubbed his cheek against it. It was breathless, and almost dead; its tongue lolled out like a rose petal that is ready to fall. In the horrified silence that encompassed the two young creatures Doña Claridad could hear the kitten panting and the child's voice murmuring:

"Pussy, poor pussy! Don't die, dear pussy, now that I've found you at last."

Walking slowly, not looking to right or left, and holding the kitten as the priest holds the pyx, he made his way through the crowd, and disappeared. Doña Claridad fell on her knees and prayed to the Mother of Sorrows.

She was still on her knees when the child came in. He was pale, and his hands were bloodstained.

"The cat is dead," he said, speaking slowly and looking at the floor. "I've killed the monkey."

Later in the day, when Don Salvador was up (for he lay late abed, having a poor constitution and little energy), Doña Claridad told him all that had happened. Speaking slowly, as Ildefonso had done, and looking at the floor, she assured him that the child had shown no horror at all, only compassion and a natural childish affection for so small and furry an animal.

"This is extraordinary! Appalling!" sighed her husband.

"It is extraordinary. But is it appalling? Is it not perhaps a grace from heaven? The child is delicate. Fits would be very bad for him."

"I cannot think it a grace from heaven that a family tradition should be set aside."

"Then is it not the grace of a reproof from heaven—a token that in the sight of God we are equal, all of us alike His sinners and His children? God is no respecter of persons. In the court of heaven the grandees of Spain must uncover like any poor peasant."

He was silent, looking at her with unhappy brows.

"You have never seen a cat, Don Salvador?"

"Never."

"It is borne in on me that you should put this grace—or this rebuke—to the test. Perhaps you too can look at a cat without trembling."

He crossed himself.

"I can deny nothing to such virtue as yours. You are my angel. I ask only one thing. Let the child be with me to give me courage."

Ildefonso was sent for. A footman carried in the dead kitten in a pair of tongs. Ildefonso looked at it calmly. Don Salvador fell down in a fit.

But no one questioned the truth of Doña Claridad. In the whole of Spain there was no honour more exquisite, no mind more heavenly, than hers.

The kitten's body was thrown on the rubbish heap, and so was the monkey's. The chaplain, in a sermon to the household, uttered a warning against giving way to gossip and vain speculation. The remaining monkeys went on catching mice, and others were trained to take the place of those that died in service. Don Salvador began to play the bass-viol and Doña Claridad continued to educate orphans, and the castle of Carabas, with its cats brandishing their paws against the sky and sometimes being grazed by lightning, enclosed the same peaceful routine, the same ways that had been current since the horn was sounded in Roncesvalles. If Don Ildefonso thought of other cats than those of the castle, he kept his thoughts to himself. He studied the Latin authors, and the laws of Spain, and wrote poetry. When he was fifteen his mother died. The old man and the young kept house together, somewhat pestered by Doña Claridad's aunt, who remained to guide the household.

One day, having looked long and fixedly at Don Ildefonso's birth-mark, Don Salvador said:

"Do you remember the kitten?"

Don Ildefonso replied that he remembered it very well.

"And you felt no horror? Strange! No horror at all, after a continuance through five generations. My son, perhaps you will think me foolish, but I cannot help feeling guilty towards you—as though I had denied or defrauded you of part of your inheritance. An inconvenient part, no doubt, yet still a family possession. When you were begotten the force of my blood was already abated. Perhaps I was too feeble to give you the whole of your inheritance. Or perhaps that part of it had already gone astray. As a young man I was no saint, unfortunately. Sometimes I ask myself whether there may not be, somewhere in Spain, somewhere even in France or Sicily, a bastard elder brother of yours who, when he sees a cat, falls down insensible."

"In five generations something may be mislaid," replied Don Ildefonso. "And you have given me the birth-mark." Then, thinking that the old man seemed melancholy, he led the conversation to family traditions and to Don Ildefonso el combatidor. Don Salvador listened with a peaceful smile, then suddenly exclaimed with energy:

"You know, those boots had spurs on them! The cat's boots, I mean. Little spurs, such as to fit one of those animals. I saw them when I was a boy. I have not seen them, though, for a long time. I wonder where they are? In the garret, perhaps. As prayers mount to heaven, rubbish mounts to the garret."

He mused and fell asleep.

Don Ildefonso decided he would look for the spurs.

He looked in the first garret, and in the second. There was nothing there he had not known as a child. Thinking that after all the spurs were probably in the muniment room, he was about to go downstairs when he was touched by a slender ray of sunlight in which the motes danced. It was small, no more than a needle of light, and slanted from the wall. He looked closer, and saw that it came through a key-hole and that the key-hole was in a narrow door. He pressed, and the door opened, and he found himself in a third garret that he had forgotten. It had a lancet window facing west, and the sun struck in like a blow on the eyes and dazzled him. Something sat on the window-sill between him and the sun. It was a large speckled cat that sat basking and did not move.

He was so much used to seeing carved cats that he thought that this, too, was a cat carved from wood and painted with speckles. But more naturalistic than the others, for it wore no boots and its expression was cold and calm.

"So there you are at last," it observed, not turning its head. He could understand its language perfectly.

"Have you been here for very long?"

"Personally, for about seven years. Long enough to know all about you. You are Don Ildefonso, the sixth in descent from Don Ildefonso el traidor. I have no name. But I am the seventy-seventh in the male line from the cat he betrayed and murdered."

It turned and looked at him. It asked sharply:

"Why aren't you in a fit?"

"I am not like my ancestor. I—I like cats."

"You like cats, do you? That's a change of heart." It spoke with assumed flippancy, but its voice was extraordinarily bitter.

"You like cats. *But I hate men!*"

Now it turned on him with bristling fur and blazing eyes. He thought it was about to spring at his throat; but after a moment it sat down again and stared at a fly in the window.

"Do you wonder?"

"Señor Don Cat, I feel I do not understand you. I am curious to know why you hate men."

"You have never heard the story, then?"

"The story of our ancestors, Señor?"

"The story of our ancestors, Señor."

With his heart thumping against his ribs, the young man explained how he had known there was a story, and had inquired after it many times, but always to no purpose.

"It is a story of human conceit and human ingratitude. Nothing very remarkable about that."

Don Ildefonso felt himself beginning to turn crimson. The birth-mark on his cheek throbbed like a heart.

"It is a story of treachery and the vilest inhospitality. It is a story that has been handed down through almost fourscore generations of my family; and each one of us in turn has taken an oath to avenge our ancestor in single combat, if and when the opportunity came. We are alone in this garret. You have your sword and I have my claws. Shall we fight it out?"

Don Ildefonso looked at the cat's furry belly. He was no coward, but he remembered the kitten and the monkey, and knew he could not fight a cat. He drew his sword from the scabbard and threw it on the floor.

The cat quivered a little as it fell clanging down. Recovering its self-control, it said:

"I might also avenge my ancestor by telling you the whole story. That would be quite as effective, I think—and would entail less exertion. Listen!"

He settled himself on the window-sill, tucked his paws under his bosom, curled his tail around, passed his tongue across his lips, and began.

The story was long and he told it minutely and composedly. There was now no malice in his voice, and presently no shade of irony, even. There was no need for such adventitious aids. As the narrative flowed onwards like a black river, its narrator seemed almost to vanish, to be no longer a personality, but instead a cloud of witnesses, a shadowy sum of seventy-seven generations, still vibrating with indignation at an intolerable piece of caddishness. Yet the recital eased him for when he had finished he sat up and shook his ears once or twice, and then sprang lightly off the window-sill and began to mountaineer about the contents of the garret.

Don Ildefonso stood waiting. It seemed to him that he must wait until the birth-mark in his cheek ceased throbbing, until he could be sure that he would not weep like a shamed child, until he could grow hardened enough to carry out his next purpose without bungling.

"I offer my apology. I can offer no reparation."

"None, none!" replied the cat briskly.

Don Ildefonso turned away.

"You've left your sword!" cried the cat, who did not resist this last scratch.

The young man walked through the outer garrets, and downstairs. Compassion for an innocent old man who was his father made it impossible for him to repeat the cat's story to Don Salvador. Instead, he merely told him that he had made up his mind to leave the world and enter the order of Carmelites. The old man sighed, vaguely as a wind in summer, and said that Doña Claridad would have approved.

A few weeks after Don Ildefonso's going Don Salvador died. For a little while the castle stood empty, then it was bought by a community of nuns. They began to scrub and clean, and soon they reached the garrets. There they found the sword, and made small jokes about it, saying that it would serve to defend them against robbers. They did not find the cat, for he had retired to an outhouse. From there he observed them until he knew them thoroughly, and felt pretty sure of them. He decided that they were clean, quiet, and of regular habits. So he began to woo them, and before winter was established among them and living very comfortably with the past behind him.

14.

The King o' the Cats

ANON.

In this old English fairy tale we are introduced to the king of the cats, and learn the strange story of how his title is passed on to the next generation. We shall meet this king again in the next selection, in a very different guise—a far more colorful character, though just as black.

ONE winter's evening the sexton's wife was sitting by the fireside with her big black cat, Old Tom, on the other side, both half asleep and waiting for the master to come home. They waited and they waited, but still he didn't come, till at last he came rushing in, calling out, "Who's Tommy Tildrum?" in such a wild way that both his wife and his cat stared at him to know what was the matter.

"Why, what's the matter?" said his wife, "and why do you want to know who Tommy Tildrum is?"

"Oh, I've had such an adventure. I was digging away at old Mr. Fordyce's grave when I suppose I must have dropped asleep, and only woke up by hearing a cat's *miaou*."

"*Miaou!*" said Old Tom in answer.

"Yes, just like that! So I looked over the edge of the grave, and what do you think I saw?"

"Now, how can I tell?" said the sexton's wife.

"Why, nine black cats all like our friend Tom here, all

with a white spot on their chestesses. And what do you think they were carrying? Why, a small coffin covered with a black velvet pall, and on the pall was a small coronet all of gold, and at every third step they took they cried all together, *miaou*—"

"*Miaou!*" said Old Tom again.

"Yes, just like that!" said the sexton. "And as they came nearer and nearer to me I could see them more distinctly, because their eyes shone out with a sort of green light. Well, they all came toward me, eight of them carrying the coffin, and the biggest cat of all walking in front for all the world like—but look at our Tom, how he's looking at me. You'd think he knew all I was saying."

"Go on, go on," said his wife, "never mind Old Tom."

"Well, as I was a-saying, they came toward me slowly, and solemnly, and at every third step crying all together, *miaou*—"

"*Miaou!*" said Old Tom again.

"Yes, just like that, till they came and stood right opposite Mr. Fordyce's grave, where I was, when they all stood still and looked straight at me. I did feel queer, that I did! But look at Old Tom—he's looking at me just like they did."

"Go on, go on," said his wife, "never mind Old Tom."

"Where was I? Oh, they all stood still looking at me, when

the one that wasn't carrying the coffin came forward and, staring straight at me, said to me—yes, I told 'ee, *said* to me, with a squeaky voice, 'Tell Tom Tildrum that Tim Toldrum's dead,' and that's why I asked you if you know who Tom Tildrum was, for how can I tell Tom Tildrum Tim Toldrum's dead if I don't know who Tom Tildrum is?"

"Look at Old Tom, look at Old Tom!" screamed his wife.

And well he might look, for Tom was swelling, and Tom was staring, and at last Tom shrieked out, "What—old Tim dead! then I'm king o' the Cats!" and rushed up the chimney and was nevermore seen.

15.

The King of the Cats

by STEPHEN VINCENT BENÉT

Stephen Vincent Benét, a member of an important American literary family, is best known for his poetry; his Civil War epic *John
Brown's Body* won him the Pulitzer Prize in 1929. On occasion he
turned his creative efforts to the short story, producing such sparkling gems of fantasy as "The Devil and Daniel Webster" and "The
King of the Cats"—an imaginative elaboration of the old legend,
which you are about to read.

"But, my *dear*," said Mrs. Culverin, with a tiny
gasp, "you can't actually mean—a *tail*!"

Mrs. Dingle nodded impressively. "Exactly. I've seen him.
Twice. Paris, of course, and then, a command appearance at
Rome—we were in the Royal box. He conducted—my dear,
you've never heard such effects from an orchestra—and, my
dear," she hesitated slightly, "he conducted *with it*."

"How perfectly, fascinatingly too horrid for words!" said
Mrs. Culverin in a dazed but greedy voice. "We *must* have
him to dinner as soon as he comes over—he is coming over,
isn't he?"

"The twelfth," said Mrs. Dingle with a gleam in her eyes.
"The New Symphony people have asked him to be guest-
conductor for three special concerts—I do hope you can dine
with *us* some night while he's here—he'll be very busy, of

course—but he's promised to give us what time he can spare—"

"Oh, thank you, dear," said Mrs. Culverin, abstractedly, her last raid upon Mrs. Dingle's pet British novelist still fresh in her mind. "You're always so delightfully hospitable —but you mustn't wear yourself out—the rest of us must do *our* part—I know Henry and myself would be only too glad to—"

"That's very sweet of you, darling." Mrs. Dingle also remembered the larceny of the British novelist. "But we're just going to give Monsieur Tibault—sweet name, isn't it! They say he's descended from the Tybalt in *Romeo and Juliet* and that's why he doesn't like Shakespeare—we're just going to give Monsieur Tibault the simplest sort of time—a little reception after his first concert, perhaps. He hates," she looked around the table, "large, mixed parties. And then, of course, his—er—little idiosyncrasy—" she coughed delicately. "It makes him feel a trifle shy with strangers."

"But I don't understand yet, Aunt Emily," said Tommy Brooks, Mrs. Dingle's nephew. "Do you really mean this Tibault bozo has a tail? Like a monkey and everything?"

"Tommy dear," said Mrs. Culverin, crushingly, "in the first place Monsieur Tibault is not a bozo—he is a very distinguished musician—the finest conductor in Europe. And in the second place—"

"He has," Mrs. Dingle was firm. "He has a tail. He conducts with it."

"Oh, but honestly!" said Tommy, his ears pinkening. "I mean, of course, if you say so, Aunt Emily. I'm sure he has —but still it sounds pretty steep, if you know what I mean! How about it, Professor Tatto?"

Professor Tatto cleared his throat. "Tck," he said, putting

his fingertips together cautiously. "I shall be very anxious to see this Monsieur Tibault. For myself, I have never observed a genuine specimen of *homo caudatus,* so I should be inclined to doubt, and yet . . . In the Middle Ages, for instance, the belief in men er—tailed or with caudal appendages of some sort, was both widespread and, as far as we can gather, well-founded. As late as the eighteenth century, a Dutch sea-captain with some character for veracity recounts the discovery of a pair of such creatures in the island of Formosa. They were in a low state of civilization, I believe, but the appendages in question were quite distinct. And in 1860, Doctor Grimbrook, the English surgeon, claims to have treated no less than three African natives with short but evident tails—though his testimony rests upon his unsupported word. After all, the thing is not impossible though doubtless unusual. Web feet—rudimentary gills—these occur with some frequency. The appendix we have with us always. The chain of our descent from the apelike form is by no means complete. For that matter," he beamed around the table, "what can we call the last few vertebrae of the normal spine but the beginnings of a concealed and rudimentary tail? Oh, yes—yes—it's possible—quite—that in an extraordinary case—a reversion to type—a survival—though, of course—"

"I told you so," said Mrs. Dingle triumphantly. "*Isn't* it fascinating. Isn't it, Princess?"

The Princess Vivrakanarda's eyes, blue as a field of larkspur, fathomless as the center of heaven, rested lightly for a moment on Mrs. Dingle's excited countenance.

"Ve-ry fascinating," she said, in a voice like stroked, golden velvet. "I should like—I should like ve-ry much to meet this Monsieur Tibault."

"Well, *I* hope he breaks his neck!" said Tommy Brooks, under his breath—but nobody ever paid much attention to Tommy.

Nevertheless as the time for M. Tibault's arrival in these States drew nearer and nearer, people in general began to wonder whether the Princess had spoken quite truthfully— for there was no doubt of the fact that, up till then, she had been the unique sensation of the season—and you know what social lions and lionesses are.

It was, if you remember, a Siamese season, and genuine Siamese were at quite as much of a premium as Russian accents had been in the quaint old days when the Chauve- Souris was a novelty. The Siamese Art Theater, imported at terrific expense, was playing to packed houses. *Gushuptzgu*, an epic novel of Siamese farm life, in nineteen closely printed volumes, had just been awarded the Nobel prize. Prominent pet-and-newt-dealers reported no cessation in the appalling demand for Siamese cats. And upon the crest of this wave of interest in things Siamese, the Princess Vivrakanarda poised with the elegant nonchalance of a Hawaiian water-baby upon its surfboard. She was indispensable. She was incomparable. She was everywhere.

Youthful, enormously wealthy, allied on one hand to the Royal Family of Siam and on the other to the Cabots (and yet with the first eighteen of her twenty-one years shrouded from speculation in a golden zone of mystery), the mingling of races in her had produced an exotic beauty as distin- guished as it was strange. She moved with a feline, effortless grace, and her skin was as if it had been gently powdered with tiny grains of the purest gold—yet the blueness of her eyes, set just a trifle slantingly, was as pure and startling as the sea on the rocks of Maine. Her brown hair fell to her knees—she had been offered extraordinary sums by the Master Barbers' Protective Association to have it shingled. Straight as a waterfall tumbling over brown rocks, it had a vague perfume of sandalwood and suave spices and held tints of rust and the sun. She did not talk very much—but then she did not have to—her voice had an odd, small, melodious huskiness that haunted the mind. She lived alone and was reputed to be very lazy—at least it was known that she slept during most of the day—but at night she bloomed like a moonflower and a depth came into her eyes.

It was no wonder that Tommy Brooks fell in love with her. The wonder was that she let him. There was nothing exotic or distinguished about Tommy—he was just one of those pleasant, normal young men who seem created to carry on the bond business by reading the newspapers in the University Club during most of the day, and can always be relied upon at night to fill an unexpected hole in a dinner party. It is true that the Princess could hardly be said to do more than tolerate any of her suitors—no one had ever seen those aloofly arrogant eyes enliven at the entrance of any male. But she seemed to be able to tolerate Tommy a little more than the rest—and that young man's infatuated day-dreams were beginning to be beset by smart solitaires and imaginary apartments on Park Avenue, when the famous M. Tibault conducted his first concert at Carnegie Hall.

Tommy Brooks sat beside the Princess. The eyes he turned upon her were eyes of longing and love, but her face was as impassive as a mask, and the only remark she made during the preliminary bustlings was that there seemed to be a number of people in the audience. But Tommy was relieved, if anything, to find her even a little more aloof than usual, for, ever since Mrs. Culverin's dinner party, a vague disquiet as to the possible impression which this Tibault creature might make upon her had been growing in his mind. It shows his devotion that he was present at all. To a man whose simple Princetonian nature found in "Just a Little Love, a Little Kiss," the quintessence of musical art, the average symphony was a positive torture, and he looked forward to the evening's programme itself with a grim brave smile.

"Ssh!" said Mrs. Dingle, breathlessly. "He's coming!" It seemed to the startled Tommy as if he were suddenly back in the trenches under a heavy barrage, as M. Tibault made his entrance to a perfect bombardment of applause.

Then the enthusiastic noise was sliced off in the middle and a gasp took its place—a vast, windy sigh, as if every person in that multitude had suddenly said, "Ah." For the papers had not lied about him. The tail was there.

They called him theatric—but how well he understood the uses of theatricalism! Dressed in unrelieved black from head to foot (the black dress-shirt had been a special token of Mussolini's esteem), he did not walk on, he strolled, lei-surely, easily, aloofly, the famous tail curled nonchalantly about one wrist—a suave, black panther lounging through a summer garden with that little mysterious weave of the head that panthers have when they pad behind bars—the glittering darkness of his eyes unmoved by any surprise or elation. He nodded, twice, in regal acknowledgment, as the clapping reached an apogee of frenzy. To Tommy there was something dreadfully reminiscent of the Princess in the way he nodded. Then he turned to his orchestra.

A second and louder gasp went up from the audience at this point, for, as he turned, the tip of that incredible tail twined with dainty carelessness into some hidden pocket and produced a black baton. But Tommy did not even notice. He was looking at the Princess instead.

She had not even bothered to clap, at first, but now—He had never seen her moved like this, never. She was not applauding, her hands were clenched in her lap, but her whole body was rigid, rigid as a steel bar, and the blue flowers of her eyes were bent upon the figure of M. Tibault in a terrible concentration. The pose of her entire figure was so still and intense that for an instant Tommy had the lunatic idea that any moment she might leap from her seat beside him as lightly as a moth, and land, with no sound, at M. Tibault's side to—yes—to rub her proud head against his coat in worship. Even Mrs. Dingle would notice in a moment.

"Princess—" he said, in a horrified whisper, "Princess—"

Slowly the tenseness of her body relaxed, her eyes veiled again, she grew calm.

"Yes, Tommy?" she said, in her usual voice, but there was still something about her . . .

"Nothing, only—oh, hang—he's starting!" said Tommy, as M. Tibault, his hands loosely clasped before him, turned and *faced* his audience. His eyes dropped, his tail switched once impressively, then gave three little preliminary taps with his baton on the floor.

Seldom has Gluck's overture to *Iphigenie in Aulis* received such an ovation. But it was not until the Eighth Symphony that the hysteria of the audience reached its climax. Never before had the New Symphony been played so superbly—and certainly never before had it been led with such genius. Three prominent conductors in the audience were sobbing with the despairing admiration of envious children toward the close, and one at least was heard to offer wildly ten thousand dollars to a well-known facial surgeon there present for a shred of evidence that tails of some variety could by any stretch of science be grafted upon a normally decaudate form. There was no doubt about it—no mortal hand and arm, be they ever so dexterous, could combine the delicate *élan* and powerful grace displayed in every gesture of M. Tibault's tail.

A sable staff, it dominated the brasses like a flicker of black lightning; an ebon, elusive whip, it drew the last exquisite breath of melody from the woodwinds and ruled the stormy strings like a magician's rod. M. Tibault bowed and bowed again—roar after roar of frenzied admiration shook the hall to its foundations—and when he finally staggered, exhausted, from the platform, the president of the Wednesday Sonata Club was only restrained by force from flinging her ninety-thousand dollar string of pearls after him in an excess of esthetic appreciation. New York had come and seen—and New York was conquered. Mrs. Dingle was immediately besieged by reporters, and Tommy Brooks looked forward to the "little party" at which he was to meet the new hero of the hour with feelings only a little less lugubrious than those that would have come to him just before taking his seat in the electric chair.

The meeting between his Princess and M. Tibault was worse and better than he expected. Better because, after all, they did not say much to each other—and worse because it seemed to him, somehow, that some curious kinship of mind between them made words unnecessary. They were certainly the most distinguished-looking couple in the room, as he bent over her hand. "So darlingly foreign, both of them, and

yet so different," babbled Mrs. Dingle—but Tommy couldn't
agree.

They were different, yes—the dark, lithe stranger with the
bizarre appendage tucked carelessly in his pocket, and the
blue-eyed, brown-haired girl. But that difference only ac-
centuated what they had in common—something in the way
they moved, in the suavity of their gestures, in the set of
their eyes. Something deeper, even, than race. He tried to
puzzle it out—then, looking around at the others, he had a
flash of revelation. It was as if that couple were foreign,
indeed—not only to New York but to all common humanity.
As if they were polite guests from a different star.

Tommy did not have a very happy evening, on the whole.
But his mind worked slowly, and it was not until much later
that the mad suspicion came upon him in full force.

Perhaps he is not to be blamed for his lack of immediate
comprehension. The next few weeks were weeks of bewildered misery for him. It was not that the Princess's attitude
toward him had changed—she was just as tolerant of him as
before, but M. Tibault was always there. He had a faculty
of appearing as out of thin air—he walked, for all his height,
as light as a butterfly—and Tommy grew to hate that faintest
shuffle on the carpet that announced his presence.

And then, hang it all, the man was so smooth, so infer-
nally, unruffably smooth! He was never out of temper, never
embarrassed. He treated Tommy with the extreme of urban-
ity, and yet his eyes mocked, deep-down, and Tommy could
do nothing. And, gradually, the Princess became more and
more drawn to this stranger, in a soundless communion that
found little need for speech—and that, too, Tommy saw and
hated, and that, too, he could not mend.

He began to be haunted not only by M. Tibault in the

flesh, but by M. Tibault in the spirit. He slept badly, and when he slept, he dreamed—of M. Tibault, a man no longer, but a shadow, a specter, the limber ghost of an animal whose words came purringly between sharp little pointed teeth. There was certainly something odd about the whole shape of the fellow—his fluid ease, the mould of his head, even the cut of his fingernails—but just what it was escaped Tommy's intensest cogitation. And when he did put his finger on it at length, at first he refused to believe.

A pair of petty incidents decided him, finally, against all reason. He had gone to Mrs. Dingle's, one winter afternoon, hoping to find the Princess. She was out with his aunt, but was expected back for tea, and he wandered idly into the library to wait. He was just about to switch on the lights, for the library was always dark even in summer, when he heard a sound of light breathing that seemed to come from the leather couch in the corner. He approached it cautiously and dimly made out the form of M. Tibault, curled upon the couch, peacefully asleep.

The sight annoyed Tommy so that he swore under his breath and was back near the door on his way out, when the feeling we all know and hate, the feeling that eyes we cannot see are watching us, arrested him. He turned back—M. Tibault had not moved a muscle of his body to all appearance—but his eyes were open now. And those eyes were black and human no longer. They were green—Tommy could have sworn that they had no bottom and gleamed like little emeralds in the dark. It only lasted a moment, for Tommy pressed the light-button automatically—and there was M. Tibault, his normal self, yawning a little but urbanely apologetic, but it gave Tommy time to think. Nor did what happened a trifle later increase his peace of mind.

They had lit a fire and were talking in front of it—by now Tommy hated M. Tibault so thoroughly that he felt that odd yearning for his company that often occurs in such cases. M. Tibault was telling some anecdote and Tommy was hating him worse than ever for basking with such obvious enjoyment in the heat of the flames and the ripple of his own voice.

Then they heard the street-door open, and M. Tibault jumped up—and jumping, caught one sock on a sharp corner of the brass fire-rail and tore it open in a jagged flap. Tommy looked down mechanically at the tear—a second's glance, but enough—for M. Tibault, for the first time in Tommy's experience, lost his temper completely. He swore violently in some spitting, foreign tongue—his face distorted suddenly— he clapped his hand over his sock. Then, glaring furiously at Tommy, he fairly sprang from the room, and Tommy could hear him scaling the stairs in long, agile bounds.

Tommy sank into a chair, careless for once of the fact that he heard the Princess's light laugh in the hall. He didn't want to see the Princess. He didn't want to see anybody. There had been something revealed when M. Tibault had torn that hole in his sock—and it was not the skin of a man. Tommy had caught a glimpse of—black plush. Black velvet. And then had come M. Tibault's sudden explosion of fury. Good *Lord*—did the man wear black velvet stockings under his ordinary socks? Or could he—could he—but here Tommy held his fevered head in his hands.

He went to Professor Tatto that evening with a series of hypothetical questions, but as he did not dare confide his real suspicions to the Professor, the hypothetical answers he received served only to confuse him the more. Then he thought of Billy Strange. Billy was a good sort, and his mind had a turn for the bizarre. Billy might be able to help.

He couldn't get hold of Billy for three days and lived through the interval in a fever of impatience. But finally they had dinner together at Billy's apartment, where his queer books were, and Tommy was able to blurt out the whole disordered jumble of his suspicions.

Billy listened without interrupting until Tommy was quite through. Then he pulled at his pipe. "But my dear *man*—" he said, protestingly.

"Oh, I know—I know—" said Tommy, and waved his hands, "I know I'm crazy—you needn't tell me that—but I tell you, the man's a cat all the same—no, I don't see how he could be, but he is—why, hang it, in the first place, everybody knows he's got a tail!"

"Even so," said Billy, puffing. "Oh, my dear Tommy, I don't doubt you saw, or think you saw, everything you say. But, even so—" He shook his head.

"But what about those other birds, werewolves and things?" said Tommy.

Billy looked dubious. "We-ll," he admitted, "you've got me there, of course. At least—a tailed man *is* possible. And the yarns about werewolves go back far enough, so that— well, I wouldn't say there aren't or haven't been werewolves —but then I'm willing to believe more things than most people. But a werecat—or a man that's a cat and a cat that's a man—honestly, Tommy—"

"If I don't get some real advice I'll go clean off my hinge. For Heaven's sake, tell me something to *do*!"

"Lemme think," said Billy. "First, you're pizen-sure this man is—"

"A cat. Yeah." And Tommy nodded violently.

"Check. And second—if it doesn't hurt your feelings, Tommy—you're afraid this girl you're in love with has—er —at least a streak of—felinity—in her—and so she's drawn to him?"

"Oh, Lord, Billy, if I only knew!"

"Well—er—suppose she really is, too, you know—would you still be keen on her?"

"I'd marry her if she turned into a dragon every Wednesday!" said Tommy, fervently.

Billy smiled. "H'm," he said, "then the obvious thing to do is to get rid of this M. Tibault. Lemme think."

He thought about two pipes full, while Tommy sat on pins and needles. Then, finally, he burst out laughing.

"What's so darn funny?" said Tommy, aggrievedly.

"Nothing, Tommy, only I've just thought of a stunt—something so blooming crazy—but if he is—h'm—what you think he is—it *might* work—" And, going to the bookcase, he took down a book.

"If you think you're going to quiet my nerves by reading me a bedtime story—"

"Shut up, Tommy, and listen to this—if you really want to get rid of your feline friend."

"What is it?"

"Book of Agnes Repplier's. About cats. Listen."

" 'There is also a Scandinavian version of the ever famous story which Sir Walter Scott told to Washington Irving, which Monk Lewis told to Shelley and which, in one form or another, we find embodied in the folklore of every land'—now, Tommy, pay attention—'the story of the traveler who saw within a ruined abbey a procession of cats lowering into a grave a little coffin with a crown upon it. Filled with horror, he hastened from the spot; but when he had reached his destination, he could not forbear relating to a friend the wonder he had seen. Scarcely had the tale been told when his friend's cat, who lay curled up tranquilly by the fire, sprang to its feet, cried out, "Then I am the King of the Cats!" and disappeared in a flash up the chimney.' "

"Well?" said Billy, shutting the book.

"By gum!" said Tommy, staring. "By gum! Do you think there's a chance?"

"*I* think we're both in the booby-hatch. But if you want to try it—"

"Try it! I'll spring it on him the next time I see him. But—listen—I can't make it a ruined abbey—"

"Oh, use your imagination! Make it Central Park—anywhere. Tell it as if it happened to you—seeing the funeral procession and all that. You can lead into it somehow—let's see—some general line—oh, yes— 'Strange, isn't it, how fact so often copies fiction. Why, only yesterday—' See?"

"Strange, isn't it, how fact so often copies fiction," repeated Tommy dutifully. "Why, only yesterday—"

"I happened to be strolling through Central Park when I saw something very odd."

"I happened to be strolling through—here, gimme that book!" said Tommy, "I want to learn the rest of it by heart!"

Mrs. Dingle's farewell dinner to the famous Monsieur Tibault, on the occasion of his departure for his Western tour, was looked forward to with the greatest expectations. Not only would everybody be there, including the Princess Vivrakanarda, but Mrs. Dingle, a hinter if there ever was one, had let it be known that at this dinner an announcement of very unusual interest to Society might be made. So everyone, for once, was almost on time, except for Tommy. He was at least fifteen minutes early, for he wanted to have speech with his aunt alone. Unfortunately, however, he had hardly taken off his overcoat when she was whispering some news in his ear so rapidly that he found it difficult to understand a word of it.

"And you mustn't breathe it to a soul!" she ended, beaming. "That is, not before the announcement—I think we'll have *that* with the salad—people never pay very much attention to salad—"

"Breathe what, Aunt Emily?" said Tommy, confused.

"The Princess, darling—the dear Princess and Monsieur Tibault—they just got engaged this afternoon, dear things! Isn't it *fascinating*?"

"Yeah," said Tommy, and started to walk blindly through the nearest door. His aunt restrained him.

"Not there, dear—not in the library. You can congratulate them later. They're just having a sweet little moment alone there now—" And she turned away to harry the butler, leaving Tommy stunned.

But his chin came up after a moment. He wasn't beaten yet.

"Strange, isn't it, how often fact copies fiction?" he repeated to himself in dull mnemonics, and, as he did so, he shook his fist at the library door.

Mrs. Dingle was wrong, as usual. The Princess and M. Tibault were not in the library—they were in the conservatory, as Tommy discovered when he wandered aimlessly past the glass doors.

He didn't mean to look, and after a second he turned away. But that second was enough.

Tibault was seated in a chair and she was crouched on a

stool at his side, while his hand, softly, smoothly, stroked her brown hair. Black cat and Siamese kitten. Her face was hidden from Tommy, but he could see Tibault's face. And he could hear.

They were not talking, but there was a sound between them. A warm and contented sound like the murmur of giant bees in a hollow tree—a golden, musical rumble, deep-throated, that came from Tibault's lips and was answered by hers—a golden purr.

Tommy found himself back in the drawing-room, shaking hands with Mrs. Culverin, who said, frankly, that she had seldom seen him look so pale.

The first two courses of the dinner passed Tommy like dreams, but Mrs. Dingle's cellar was notable, and by the middle of the meat course, he began to come to himself. He had only one resolve now.

For the next few moments he tried desperately to break into the conversation, but Mrs. Dingle was talking, and even Gabriel will have a time interrupting Mrs. Dingle. At last, though, she paused for breath and Tommy saw his chance.

"Speaking of that," said Tommy, piercingly, without knowing in the least what he was referring to, "speaking of that—"

"As I was saying," said Professor Tatto. But Tommy would not yield. The plates were being taken away. It was time for salad.

"Speaking of that," he said again, so loudly and strangely that Mrs. Culverin jumped and an awkward hush fell over the table. "Strange, isn't it, how often fact copies fiction?" There, he was started. His voice rose even higher. "Why, only today I was strolling through—" and, word for word, he repeated his lesson. He could see Tibault's eyes glowing at him, as he described the funeral. He could see the Princess, tense.

He could not have said what he had expected might happen when he came to the end; but it was not bored silence, everywhere, to be followed by Mrs. Dingle's acrid, "Well, Tommy, is that *quite* all?"

He slumped back in his chair, sick at heart. He was a fool and his last resource had failed. Dimly he heard his aunt's voice, saying, "Well, then—" and realized that she was about to make the fatal announcement.

But just then Monsieur Tibault spoke.

"One moment, Mrs. Dingle," he said, with extreme politeness, and she was silent. He turned to Tommy.

"You are—positive, I suppose, of what you saw this afternoon, Brooks?" he said, in tones of light mockery.

"Absolutely," said Tommy sullenly. "Do you think I'd—"

"Oh, no, no, no," Monsieur Tibault waved the implication aside, "but—such an interesting story—one likes to be sure of the details—and, of course, you *are* sure—*quite* sure —that the kind of crown you describe was on the coffin?"

"Of course," said Tommy, wondering, "but—"

"Then I'm the King of the Cats!" cried Monsieur Tibault in a voice of thunder, and, even as he cried it, the house lights blinked—there was the soft thud of an explosion that seemed muffled in cotton-wool from the minstrel gallery— and the scene was lit for a second by an obliterating and painful burst of light that vanished in an instant and was succeeded by heavy, blinding clouds of white, pungent smoke.

"Oh, those *horrid* photographers," came Mrs. Dingle's voice in a melodious wail. "I *told* them not to take the flashlight picture till dinner was over, and now they've taken it *just* as I was nibbling lettuce!"

Someone tittered a little nervously. Someone coughed. Then, gradually the veils of smoke dislimned and the green-and-black spots in front of Tommy's eyes died away.

They were blinking at each other like people who have just come out of a cave into brilliant sun. Even yet their eyes stung with the fierceness of that abrupt illumination and Tommy found it hard to make out the faces across the table from him.

Mrs. Dingle took command of the half-blinded company with her accustomed poise. She rose, glass in hand. "And now, dear friends," she said in a clear voice, "I'm sure all of us are very happy to—" Then she stopped, open-mouthed, an expression of incredulous horror on her features. The lifted glass began to spill its contents on the tablecloth in a little stream of amber. As she spoke, she had turned directly to Monsieur Tibault's place at the table—and Monsieur Tibault was no longer there.

Some say there was a bursting flash of fire that disappeared up the chimney—some say it was a giant cat that leaped through the window at a bound, without breaking the glass. Professor Tatto puts it down to a mysterious chemical disturbance operating only over M. Tibault's chair. The butler, who is pious, believes the Devil in person flew away with him, and Mrs. Dingle hesitates between witchcraft and a malicious ectoplasm dematerializing on the wrong cosmic plane. But be that as it may, one thing is certain—in the instant of fictive darkness which followed the glare of the flashlight, Monsieur Tibault, the great conductor, disappeared forever from mortal sight, tail and all.

Mrs. Culverin swears he was an international burglar and that she was just about to unmask him, when he slipped away under cover of the flashlight smoke, but no one else who sat at that historic dinner table believes her. No, there are no sound explanations, but Tommy thinks he knows, and he will never be able to pass a cat again without wondering.

Mrs. Tommy is quite of her husband's mind regarding cats—she was Gretchen Woolwine, of Chicago—for Tommy told her his whole story, and while she doesn't believe a great deal of it, there is no doubt in her heart that one person concerned in the affair was a *perfect* cat. Doubtless it would have been more romantic to relate how Tommy's daring finally won him his Princess—but, unfortunately, it would not be veracious. For the Princess Vivrakanarda, also, is with us no longer. Her nerves, shattered by the spectacular denouement of Mrs. Dingle's dinner, required a sea voyage, and from that voyage she has never returned to America.

Of course, there are the usual stories—one hears of her, a nun in a Siamese convent, or a masked dancer at Le Jardin de ma Soeur—one hears that she has been murdered in Patagonia or married in Trebizond—but, as far as can be ascertained, not one of these gaudy fables has the slightest basis of fact. I believe that Tommy, in his heart of hearts, is quite convinced that the sea voyage was only a pretext, and that by some unheard-of means, she has managed to rejoin the formidable Monsieur Tibault, wherever in the world of the visible or the invisible he may be—in fact, that in some ruined city or subterranean palace they reign together now, King and Queen of all the mysterious Kingdom of Cats. But that, of course, is quite impossible.

16.

Hodge, the Cat

by SUSAN COOLIDGE

Burly and big his books among,
    Good Samuel Johnson sat,
With frowning brows and wig askew,
His snuff-strewn waistcoat far from new;
So stern and menacing his air,
  That neither "Black Sam" nor the maid
To knock or interrupt him dare;
   Yet close beside him, unafraid,
    Sat Hodge, the cat.

"This participle," the Doctor wrote,
    "The modern scholar cavils at,
But,"—even as he penned the word,
A soft protesting note was heard:
The Doctor fumbled with his pen,
  The dawning thought took wings and flew,
The sound repeated came again,
  It was a faint reminding "Mew!"
    From Hodge, the cat.

"Poor Pussy!" said the learned man,
    Giving the glossy fur a pat,
"It is your dinner time, I know,
And,—well, perhaps I ought to go;
For if Sam every day were sent
  Off from his work your fish to buy,
Why, men are men, he might resent,
   And starve or kick you on the sly;
    Eh! Hodge, my cat?"

The Dictionary was laid down,
    The Doctor tied his vast cravat,
And down the buzzing street he strode,
Taking an often-trodden road,
And halted at a well-known stall:
  "Fishmonger," spoke the Doctor gruff,
"Give me six oysters, that is all;
  Hodge knows when he has had enough,
    Hodge is my cat."

Then home; Puss dined, and while in sleep
    He chased a visionary rat,
His master sat him down again,
Rewrote his page, renibbed his pen;
Each i was dotted, each t was crossed,
    He laboured on for all to read,
Nor deemed that time was waste or lost
    Spent in supplying the small need
        Of Hodge, the cat.

The dear old Doctor! fierce of mien,
    Untidy, arbitrary, fat,
What gentle thoughts his name enfold!
So generous of his scanty gold,
So quick to love, so hot to scorn,
    Kind to all sufferers under heaven,
A tenderer despot ne'er was born;
    His big heart held a corner even
        For Hodge, the cat.

17.

Space-Time for Springers

by FRITZ LEIBER

Fritz Leiber, the son of a famed Shakespearean actor and at heart a frustrated actor himself, is a majestically tall man with a magnificent resonant voice. His fame for more than thirty years has derived from his many excellent stories of fantasy and science fiction, which have won him a loyal following. An element of the macabre exists at the heart of many of Leiber's stories—we penetrate a seemingly innocent exterior to find a subtle tone of horror beneath. "Space-Time for Springers" is no exception, as we will discover as Gummitch proceeds to instruct us in the intricacies of the space-time continuum.

GUMMITCH was a superkitten, as he knew very well, with an I.Q. of about 160. Of course, he didn't talk. But everybody knows that I.Q. tests based on language ability are very one-sided. Besides, he would talk as soon as they started setting a place for him at table and pouring him coffee. Ashurbanipal and Cleopatra ate horsemeat from pans on the floor and they didn't talk. Baby dined in his crib on milk from a bottle and he didn't talk. Sissy sat at table but they didn't pour her coffee and she didn't talk—not one word. Father and Mother (whom Gummitch had nicknamed Old Horsemeat and Kitty-Come-Here) sat at table and poured each other coffee and they *did* talk. Q. E. D.

Meanwhile, he would get by very well on thought projection and intuitive understanding of all human speech—not even to mention cat patois, which almost any civilized animal could play by ear. The dramatic monologues and Socratic dialogues, the quiz and panel-show appearances, the felidological expedition to darkest Africa (where he would uncover the real truth behind lions and tigers), the exploration of the outer planets—all these could wait. The same went for the books for which he was ceaselessly accumulating material: *The Encyclopedia of Odors, Anthropofeline Psychology, Invisible Signs and Secret Wonders, Space-Time for Springers, Slit Eyes Look at Life,* et cetera. For the present it was enough to live existence to the hilt and soak up knowledge, missing no experience proper to his age level— to rush about with tail aflame.

So to all outward appearances Gummitch was just a vividly normal kitten, as shown by the succession of nicknames he bore along the magic path that led from blue-eyed infancy toward puberty: Little One, Squawker, Portly, Bumble (for purring not clumsiness), Old Starved-to-Death, Fierso, Lover-boy (affection not sex), Spook and Catnik. Of these only the last perhaps requires further explanation: the Russians had just sent Muttnik up after Sputnik, so that

when one evening Gummitch streaked three times across the firmament of the living room floor in the same direction, past the fixed stars of the humans and the comparatively slow-moving heavenly bodies of the two older cats, and Kitty-Come-Here quoted the line from Keats:

> Then felt I like some watcher of the skies
> When a new planet swims into his ken;

it was inevitable that Old Horsemeat would say, "Ah—Cat-nik!"

The new name lasted all of three days, to be replaced by Gummitch, which showed signs of becoming permanent.

The little cat was on the verge of truly growing up, at least so Gummitch overheard Old Horsemeat comment to Kitty-Come-Here. A few short weeks, Old Horsemeat said, and Gummitch's fiery flesh would harden, his slim neck thicken, the electricity vanish from everything but his fur, and all his delightful kittenish qualities rapidly give way to the earth-bound singlemindedness of a tom. They'd be lucky, Old Horsemeat concluded, if he didn't turn completely surly like Ashurbanipal.

Gummitch listened to these predictions with gay uncon-cern and with secret amusement from his vantage point of superior knowledge, in the same spirit that he accepted so many phases of his outwardly conventional existence: the murderous sidelong looks he got from Ashurbanipal and Cleopatra as he devoured his own horsemeat from his own little tin pan, because they sometimes were given canned cat-food but he never; the stark idiocy of Baby, who didn't know the difference between a live cat and a stuffed teddy bear and who tried to cover up his ignorance by making goo-goo noises and poking indiscriminately at all eyes; the far more serious—because cleverly hidden—maliciousness of Sissy, who had to be watched out for warily—especially when you were alone—and whose retarded—even warped—development, Gummitch knew, was Old Horsemeat and Kitty-Come-Here's deepest, most secret, worry (more of Sissy and her evil ways soon); the limited intellect of Kitty-Come-Here, who despite the amounts of coffee she drank was quite as featherbrained as kittens are supposed to be and who firmly believed, for example, that kittens operated in the same space-time as other beings —that to get from *here* to *there* they had to cross the space between—and similar fallacies; the mental stodginess of even Old Horsemeat, who although he understood quite a bit of the secret doctrine and talked intelligently to Gummitch when they were alone, nevertheless suffered from the limitations of his status—a rather nice old god but a maddeningly slow-witted one.

But Gummitch could easily forgive all this massed inadequacy and downright brutishness in his felino-human household, because he was aware that he alone knew the real truth about himself and about other kittens and babies as well, the truth which was hidden from weaker minds, the truth that was as intrinsically incredible as the germ theory of disease or the origin of the whole great universe in the explosion of a single atom.

As a baby kitten Gummitch had believed that Old Horsemeat's two hands were hairless kittens permanently attached to the ends of Old Horsemeat's arms but having an independent life of their own. How he had hated and loved those two five-legged sallow monsters, his first playmates, comforters and battle-opponents!

Well, even that fantastic discarded notion was but a trifling fancy compared to the real truth about himself!

The forehead of Zeus split open to give birth to Minerva. Gummitch had been born from the waist-fold of a dirty old terrycloth bathrobe, Old Horsemeat's basic garment. The kitten was intuitively certain of it and had proved it to himself as well as any Descartes or Aristotle. In a kitten-size tuck of that ancient bathrobe the atoms of his body had gathered and quickened into life. His earliest memories were of snoozing wrapped in terrycloth, warmed by Old Horsemeat's heat. Old Horsemeat and Kitty-Come-Here were his true parents. The other theory of his origin, the one he heard Old Horsemeat and Kitty-Come-Here recount from time to time —that he had been the only surviving kitten of a litter abandoned next door, that he had had the shakes from vitamin deficiency and lost the tip of his tail and the hair on his paws and had to be nursed back to life and health with warm yellowish milk-and-vitamins fed from an eyedropper —that other theory was just one of those rationalizations with which mysterious nature cloaks the birth of heroes, perhaps wisely veiling the truth from minds unable to bear it, a rationalization as false as Kitty-Come-Here and Old Horsemeat's touching belief that Sissy and Baby were their children rather than the cubs of Ashurbanipal and Cleopatra.

The day that Gummitch had discovered by pure intuition the secret of his birth he had been filled with a wild instant excitement. He had only kept it from tearing him to pieces by rushing out to the kitchen and striking and devouring a fried scallop, torturing it fiendishly first for twenty minutes.

And the secret of his birth was only the beginning. His intellectual faculties aroused, Gummitch had two days later intuited a further and greater secret: since he was the child of humans he would, upon reaching this maturation date of which Old Horsemeat had spoken, turn not into a sullen tom but into a godlike human youth with reddish golden hair the color of his present fur. He would be poured coffee; and he would instantly be able to talk, probably in all languages. While Sissy (how clear it was now!) would at approximately the same time shrink and fur out into a sharp-clawed and vicious she-cat dark as her hair, sex and self-love her only concerns, fit harem-mate for Cleopatra, concubine to Ashurbanipal.

Exactly the same was true, Gummitch realized at once, for all kittens and babies, all humans and cats, wherever they might dwell. Metamorphosis was as much a part of the fabric of their lives as it was of the insects. It was also the basic fact underlying all legends of werewolves, vampires and witches' familiars.

If you just rid your mind of preconceived notions, Gummitch told himself, it was all very logical. Babies were stupid, fumbling, vindictive creatures without reason or speech. What more natural than that they should grow up into mute sullen selfish beasts bent only on rapine and reproduction? While kittens were quick, sensitive, subtle, supremely alive. What other destiny were they possibly fitted for except to become the deft, word-speaking, book-writing, music-making, meat-getting-and-dispensing masters of the world? To dwell on the physical differences, to point out that kittens and men, babies and cats, are rather unlike in appearance and size, would be to miss the forest for the trees—very much as if an entomologist should proclaim metamorphosis a myth because his microscope failed to discover the wings of a butterfly in a caterpillar's slime or that of a golden beetle in a grub.

Nevertheless it was such a mind-staggering truth, Gummitch realized at the same time, that it was easy to understand why humans, cats, babies and perhaps most kittens were quite unaware of it. How safely explain to a butterfly that he was once a hairy crawler, or to a dull larva that he will one day be a walking jewel? No, in such situations the delicate minds of man- and feline-kind are guarded by a merciful mass amnesia, such as Velikovsky has explained prevents us from recalling that in historical times the Earth was catastrophically bumped by the planet Venus operating in the manner of a comet before settling down (with a cosmic sigh of relief, surely!) into its present orbit.

This conclusion was confirmed when Gummitch in the first fever of illumination tried to communicate his great insight to others. He told it in cat patois, as well as that limited jargon permitted, to Ashurbanipal and Cleopatra and even, on the off chance, to Sissy and Baby. They showed no interest whatever, except that Sissy took advantage of his unguarded preoccupation to stab him with a fork.

Later, alone with Old Horsemeat, he projected the great new thoughts, staring with solemn yellow eyes at the old god, but the latter grew markedly nervous and even showed signs of real fear, so Gummitch desisted. ("You'd have sworn he was trying to put across something as deep as the Einstein theory or the doctrine of original sin," Old Horsemeat later told Kitty-Come-Here.)

But Gummitch was a man now in all but form, the kitten reminded himself after these failures, and it was part of his destiny to shoulder secrets alone when necessary. He wondered if the general amnesia would affect him when he metamorphosed. There was no sure answer to this question, but he hoped not—and sometimes felt that there was reason for his hopes. Perhaps he would be the first true kitten-man, speaking from a wisdom that had no locked doors in it.

Once he was tempted to speed up the process by the use of drugs. Left alone in the kitchen, he sprang onto the table and started to lap up the black puddle in the bottom of Old Horsemeat's coffee cup. It tasted foul and poisonous and he withdrew with a little snarl, frightened as well as revolted. The dark beverage would not work its tongue-loosening magic, he realized, except at the proper time and with the proper ceremonies. Incantations might be necessary as well. Certainly unlawful tasting was highly dangerous.

The futility of expecting coffee to work any wonders by it-self was further demonstrated to Gummitch when Kitty-Come-Here, wordlessly badgered by Sissy, gave a few spoon-fuls to the little girl, liberally lacing it first with milk and sugar. Of course Gummitch knew by now that Sissy was de-stined shortly to turn into a cat and that no amount of coffee would ever make her talk, but it was nevertheless instruc-tive to see how she spat out the first mouthful, drooling a lot of saliva after it, and dashed the cup and its contents at the chest of Kitty-Come-Here.

Gummitch continued to feel a great deal of sympathy for his parents in their worries about Sissy and he longed for the day when he would metamorphose and be able as an ac-knowledged man-child truly to console them. It was heart-

breaking to see how they each tried to coax the little girl to talk, always attempting it while the other was absent, how they seized on each accidentally wordlike note in the few sounds she uttered and repeated it back to her hopefully, how they were more and more possessed by fears not so much of her retarded (they thought) development as of her increasingly obvious maliciousness, which was directed chiefly at Baby . . . though the two cats and Gummitch bore their share. Once she had caught Baby alone in his crib and used the sharp corner of a block to dot Baby's large-domed lightly-downed head with triangular red marks. Kitty-Come-Here had discovered her doing it, but the woman's first action had been to rub Baby's head to obliterate the marks so that Old Horsemeat wouldn't see them. That was the night Kitty-Come-Here hid the abnormal psychology books.

Gummitch understood very well that Kitty-Come-Here and Old Horsemeat, honestly believing themselves to be Sissy's parents, felt just as deeply about her as if they actually were and he did what little he could under the present circumstances to help them. He had recently come to feel a quite independent affection for Baby—the miserable little proto-cat was so completely stupid and defenseless—and so he unofficially constituted himself the creature's guardian, taking his naps behind the door of the nursery and dashing about noisily whenever Sissy showed up. In any case he realized that as a potentially adult member of a felino-human household he had his natural responsibilities.

Accepting responsibilities was as much a part of a kitten's life, Gummitch told himself, as shouldering unsharable intuitions and secrets, the number of which continued to grow from day to day.

There was, for instance, the Affair of the Squirrel Mirror.

Gummitch had early solved the mystery of ordinary mirrors and of the creatures that appeared in them. A little observation and sniffing and one attempt to get behind the heavy wall-job in the living room had convinced him that mirror beings were insubstantial or at least hermetically sealed into their other world, probably creatures of pure spirit, harmless imitative ghosts—including the silent Gummitch Double who touched paws with him so softly yet so coldly.

Just the same, Gummitch had let his imagination play with what would happen if one day, while looking into the mirror world, he should let loose his grip on his spirit and let it slip into the Gummitch Double while the other's spirit slipped into his body—if, in short, he should change places with the scentless ghost kitten. Being doomed to a life consisting wholly of imitation and completely lacking in opportunities to show initiative—except for the behind-the-scenes judgment and speed needed in rushing from one mirror to another to keep up with the real Gummitch—would be sickeningly dull, Gummitch decided, and he resolved to keep a tight hold on his spirit at all times in the vicinity of mirrors.

But that isn't telling about the Squirrel Mirror. One morning Gummitch was peering out the front bedroom window that overlooked the roof of the porch. Gummitch had already classified windows as semi-mirrors having two kinds of space on the other side: the mirror world and that harsh region filled with mysterious and dangerously organized-sounding noises called the outer world, into which grownup humans reluctantly ventured at intervals, donning special garments for the purpose and shouting loud farewells that were meant to be reassuring but achieved just the opposite effect. The coexistence of two kinds of space presented no paradox to the kitten who carried in his mind the 27-chapter outline of *Space-Time for Springers*—indeed, it constituted one of the minor themes of the book.

This morning the bedroom was dark and the outer world was dull and sunless, so the mirror world was unusually difficult to see. Gummitch was just lifting his face toward it, nose twitching, his front paws on the sill, when what should rear up on the other side, exactly in the space that the Gummitch Double normally occupied, but a dirty brown, narrow-visaged image with savagely low forehead, dark evil walleyes, and a huge jaw filled with shovel-like teeth.

Gummitch was enormously startled and hideously frightened. He felt his grip on his spirit go limp, and without volition he teleported himself three yards to the rear, making use of that faculty for cutting corners in space-time, traveling by space-warp in fact, which was one of his powers that Kitty-Come-Here refused to believe in and that even Old Horsemeat accepted only on faith.

Then, not losing a moment, he picked himself up by his furry seat, swung himself around, dashed downstairs at top speed, sprang to the top of the sofa, and stared for several seconds at the Gummitch Double in the wall-mirror—not relaxing a muscle strand until he was completely convinced that he was still himself and had not been transformed into the nasty brown apparition that had confronted him in the bedroom window.

"Now what do you suppose brought that on?" Old Horsemeat asked Kitty-Come-Here.

Later Gummitch learned that what he had seen had been a squirrel, a savage, nut-hunting being belonging wholly to the outer world (except for forays into attics) and not at all to the mirror one. Nevertheless he kept a vivid memory of

his profound momentary conviction that the squirrel had
taken the Gummitch Double's place and been about to take
his own. He shuddered to think what would have happened
if the squirrel had been actively interested in trading spirits
with him. Apparently mirrors and mirror-situations, just as
he had always feared, were highly conducive to spirit trans-
fers. He filed the information away in the memory cabinet
reserved for dangerous, exciting and possibly useful information, such as plans for climbing straight up glass (diamond-
tipped claws!) and flying higher than the trees.

These days his thought cabinets were beginning to feel
filled to bursting and he could hardly wait for the moment
when the true rich taste of coffee, lawfully drunk, would
permit him to speak.

He pictured the scene in detail: the family gathered in
conclave at the kitchen table, Ashurbanipal and Cleopatra
respectfully watching from floor level, himself sitting erect on
chair with paws (or would they be hands?) lightly touching
his cup of thin china, while Old Horsemeat poured the thin
black steaming stream. He knew the Great Transformation
must be close at hand.

At the same time he knew that the other critical situation
in the household was worsening swiftly. Sissy, he realized
now, was far older than Baby and should long ago have
undergone her own somewhat less glamorous though equally
necessary transformation (the first tin of raw horsemeat
could hardly be as exciting as the first cup of coffee). Her
time was long overdue. Gummitch found increasing horror
in this mute vampirish being inhabiting the body of a rapidly
growing girl, though inwardly equipped to be nothing but a
most bloodthirsty she-cat. How dreadful to think of Old

Horsemeat and Kitty-Come-Here having to care all their lives for such a monster! Gummitch told himself that if any opportunity for alleviating his parents' misery should ever present itself to him, he would not hesitate for an instant.

Then one night, when the sense of Change was so burstingly strong in him that he knew tomorrow must be the Day, but when the house was also exceptionally unquiet with boards creaking and snapping, taps adrip, and curtains mysteriously rustling at closed windows (so that it was clear that the many spirit worlds including the mirror one must be pressing very close), the opportunity came to Gummitch.

Kitty-Come-Here and Old Horsemeat had fallen into especially sound, drugged sleeps, the former with a bad cold, the latter with one unhappy highball too many (Gummitch knew he had been brooding about Sissy). Baby slept too, though with uneasy whimperings and joggings—moonlight shone full on his crib past a window shade which had whirringly rolled itself up without human or feline agency. Gummitch kept vigil under the crib, with eyes closed but with wildly excited mind pressing outward to every boundary of the house and even stretching here and there into the outer world. On this night of all nights sleep was unthinkable.

Then suddenly he became aware of footsteps, footsteps so soft they must, he thought, be Cleopatra's.

No, softer than that, so soft they might be those of the Gummitch Double escaped from the mirror world at last and padding up toward him through the darkened halls. A ribbon of fur rose along his spine.

Then into the nursery Sissy came prowling. She looked slim as an Egyptian princess in her long thin yellow nightgown and as sure of herself, but the cat was very strong in her tonight, from the flat intent eyes to the dainty canine

teeth slightly bared—one look at her now would have sent
Kitty-Come-Here running for the telephone number she kept
hidden, the telephone number of the special doctor—and
Gummitch realized he was witnessing a monstrous suspen-
sion of natural law in that this being should be able to exist
for a moment without growing fur and changing round pupils for slit eyes.

He retreated to the darkest corner of the room, suppress-
ing a snarl.

Sissy approached the crib and leaned over Baby in the
moonlight, keeping her shadow off him. For a while she
gloated. Then she began softly to scratch his cheek with a
long hatpin she carried, keeping away from his eye, but just
barely. Baby awoke and saw her and Baby didn't cry. Sissy
continued to scratch, always a little more deeply. The moonlight glittered on the jeweled end of the pin.

Gummitch knew he faced a horror that could not be
countered by running about or even spitting and screeching.
Only magic could fight so obviously supernatural a manifes-
tation. And this was also no time to think of consequences,
no matter how clearly and bitterly etched they might appear
to a mind intensely awake.

He sprang up onto the other side of the crib, not uttering
a sound, and fixed his golden eyes on Sissy's in the moonlight. Then he moved forward straight at her evil face, stepping slowly, not swiftly, using his extraordinary knowledge
of the properties of space to *walk straight through her hand
and arm as they flailed the hatpin at him*. When his nose-tip
finally paused a fraction of an inch from hers his eyes had
not blinked once, and she could not look away. Then he un-
hesitatingly flung his spirit into her like a fistful of flaming
arrows and he worked the Mirror Magic.

Sissy's moonlit face, feline and terrified, was in a sense the last thing that Gummitch, the real Gummitch-kitten, ever saw in this world. For the next instant he felt himself enfolded by the foul black blinding cloud of Sissy's spirit, which his own had displaced. At the same time he heard the little girl scream, very loudly but even more distinctly, *"Mommy!"*

That cry might have brought Kitty-Come-Here out of her grave, let alone from sleep merely deep or drugged. Within seconds she was in the nursery, closely followed by Old Horsemeat, and she had caught up Sissy in her arms and the little girl was articulating the wonderful word again and again, and miraculously following it with the command— there could be no doubt, Old Horsemeat heard it too —"Hold me tight!"

Then Baby finally dared to cry. The scratches on his cheek came to attention and Gummitch, as he had known must happen, was banished to the basement amid cries of horror and loathing chiefly from Kitty-Come-Here.

The little cat did not mind. No basement would be one-tenth as dark as Sissy's spirit that now enshrouded him for always, hiding all the file drawers and the labels on all the folders, blotting out forever even the imagining of the scene of first coffee-drinking and first speech.

In a last intuition, before the animal blackness closed in utterly, Gummitch realized that the spirit, alas, is not the same thing as the consciousness and that one may lose—sacrifice— the first and still be burdened with the second.

Old Horsemeat had seen the hatpin (and hid it quickly

from Kitty-Come-Here) and so he knew that the situation was not what it seemed and that Gummitch was at the very least being made into a sort of scapegoat. He was quite apologetic when he brought the tin pans of food to the basement during the period of the little cat's exile. It was a comfort to Gummitch, albeit a small one. Gummitch told himself, in his new black halting manner of thinking, that after all a cat's best friend is his man.

From that night Sissy never turned back in her development. Within two months she had made three years' progress in speaking. She became an outstandingly bright, light-footed, high-spirited little girl. Although she never told anyone this, the moonlit nursery and Gummitch's magnified face were her first memories. Everything before that was inky blackness. She was always very nice to Gummitch in a careful sort of way. She could never stand to play the game "Owl Eyes."

After a few weeks Kitty-Come-Here forgot her fears and Gummitch once again had the run of the house. But by then the transformation Old Horsemeat had always warned about had fully taken place. Gummitch was a kitten no longer but an almost burly tom. In him it took the psychological form not of sullenness or surliness but an extreme dignity. He seemed at times rather like an old pirate brooding on treasures he would never live to dig up, shores of adventure he would never reach. And sometimes when you looked into his yellow eyes you felt that he had in him all the materials for the book *Slit Eyes Look at Life*—three or four volumes at least—although he would never write it. And that was natural when you come to think of it, for as Gummitch knew very well, bitterly well indeed, his fate was to be the only kitten in the world that did not grow up to be a man.

18.

An Encounter

by THÉOPHILE GAUTIER

Théophile Gautier was a French poet and romantic novelist of the nineteenth century. He also wrote many masterly short stories and autobiographical sketches, and, ailurophile that he was, these are overrun with tales of the feline members of his family. Such a tale is told in "An Encounter," an excerpt from Gautier's informal autobiography *Ménagerie Intime* (1869).

ONE day a friend, who was going away for a few weeks, left his parrot in our care. The bird, homesick and unquiet, climbed to the top of his perch, and rolled his golden eyes warily, wrinkling the white membrane which served for eyelids. My cat, Madame Théophile, had never before seen a parrot, and this strange creature filled her with amazement. Motionless as a cat mummy in its swathing bands, she fixed a profoundly meditative gaze upon the stranger, summoning to her aid all the notions of natural history which she had picked up on the roofs and in the garden. The shadow of her thoughts passed over her changing eyes, and we could read in them the results of her scrutiny: "Decidedly it is a green chicken."

This much ascertained, the cat leaped from the table which she had made her observatory, and crouched low in a corner of the room, flattening herself on the ground, like

Gérome's black panther which watches the gazelles coming down to drink from the lake. The parrot followed her movements with feverish anxiety. He ruffled his feathers, shook his chain, raised one claw after another, and whetted his beak on the side of his drinking cup. Instinct told him that here was an enemy plotting mischief. The cat's eyes were all this time fixed upon the bird with terrible intensity, and they said in a language which the poor parrot but too plainly understood: "Green though it be, this chicken is doubtless very good to eat."

We watched the little drama with interest, ready to intervene at need. Madame Théophile crept slowly, almost imperceptibly, forward. Her pink nose quivered, her eyes were half closed, her claws moved in and out of their soft sheaths, little tremors of rapture ran along her spine. She was like an epicure sitting down to a chicken and truffles. Such a novel and exotic fare tempted her gluttony.

Suddenly her back bent like a bow, and with a vigorous spring she leaped upon the perch. The parrot, seeing the imminence of his peril, cried in a voice as deep and vibrating as M. Prudhomme's: "Hast thou breakfasted, Jacquot?"

The utterance so terrified the cat that she fell backwards. The blare of a trumpet, the crash of crockery, the report of a pistol could not have made her more dizzy with fright. All her ornithological theories were overthrown.

"And on what? On the king's roast?" continued the parrot.

Then we, the observers, read in the expressive countenance of Madame Théophile: "This is not a bird; it speaks; it is a gentleman." Questioningly the cat looked at me. My answer proving unsatisfactory, she crawled under the bed and refused to come out for the rest of the day.

19.

Practice

by HIPPOLYTE TAINE

Cultivate your garden, said Goethe and Voltaire,
Every other task is wasted and dead-born;
Narrow all your efforts to a given sphere,
Seek your Heaven daily in a bit of ground.

So my cat behaves. Like a veteran,
He brushes well his coat before he sits to dine;
All his work is centered in his own domain,
Just to keep his spotless fur soft, and clean, and fine.

His tongue is sponge, and brush, and towel, and curry-comb,
Well he knows what work it can be made to do,
Poor little wash-rag, smaller than my thumb.

His nose touches his back, touches his hind paws too,
Every patch of fur is raked, and scraped, and smoothed;
What more has Goethe done, what more could Voltaire do?

20.

The Chelsea Cat

by C. H. B. KITCHIN

"The Chelsea Cat" is a real honest-to-goodness modern ghost story, and lucky are we that it is also a cat story—two cat stories, in fact, for in addition to the Chelsea Cat there is Tompkins . . . for a while. C. H. B. Kitchin weaves richly portrayed characters through a web of wild and wonderful events as the tale of this porcelain prize unwinds to its inevitable conclusion.

Mʀ. Mallowbourne had made all his arrangements. He would reach Scotties' sale-room in time for lot 90, put in a few halfhearted bids for lot 98, a late Vienna coffee-service, and having failed to get it, retire to the background with a crest-fallen air and listen to the bidding—especially to the bidding for lot 105. Nobody but his confidential agent, Mr. Rebus, would know that his real interest lay there. And then—one must make no rash predictions, but money was tight, a more than usually gloomy budget impended and Labour threatened to lay its uncouth hands on capital—the very sinews of a worth-while civilization. It would be surprising indeed if Mr. Mallowbourne didn't become the new owner of the Chelsea Cat.

He had first seen it in the Hooper-Hoade collection a few years before. He had known Hooper-Hoade slightly, but hadn't taken to him—an astute collector, but an aggressive

man with little charm of manner. Mr. Mallowbourne remembered him pointing to the Cat with his thumb and saying, "Now this is one of my real treasures," with a touch of
acquired American twang overlaying his native Lancashire.

Mr. Mallowbourne would never have pointed—least of all
with his thumb. The Cat would be sitting complacently in
its cabinet, but he would say nothing about it, unless you
questioned him. Then he would tell you, with a modest
avoidance both of pedantry and possessiveness, "Cats are
rare. Chelsea produced relatively few animal-figures in the
early years of the Red Anchor period—that is to say, the
period from which most of my Chelsea specimens are supposed to date—and though you may find monkeys and sheep
and cows and of course dogs, you'll have to search quite hard
before you find a cat." And if you seemed to be interested
enough he would go on to tell you how the Englishman's
tendency to lavish sentimentality on dogs (which both pan-
dered to his blood-lust in the chase and flattered his vanity
in the home) was destined to cumber the chimney-pieces of
England with crude earthenware reproductions of that over-
rated and insanitary animal. Chelsea dogs were admittedly a
different matter, and Chelsea dogs of the Red Anchor period
a more different matter still, while as for Chelsea cats, well,
people who should know said that this was the earliest known
specimen.

Mr. Mallowbourne was very English, but he happened to

dislike dogs even more than he disliked most animals, and in this little lecture (which we must confess he had been preparing ever since he had decided to acquire the Chelsea Cat) he couldn't refrain from airing his prejudice.

On the night before the sale he went to sleep with the sale-catalogue on the table by his bed. It opened, needless to say, at the Cat's picture. "See lot 105 for a description of this earliest known example of a Chelsea Cat. From the collection of the late R. Hooper-Hoade Esq." And in his last waking moment, he murmured to himself a line from an imaginary poem:

Dear Puss shall purr me through a ripe old age . . .

2

His awakening the next morning was a rude contrast. It came to him suddenly in the middle of a nightmare, and when he opened his eyes to be half blinded by a baneful steel-grey light, someone or something was beating into his brain the words, "You must not buy the Chelsea Cat." This was all he could remember, but it was enough to fill him with a bleak and horrible dismay. Try as he would, he couldn't laugh it off or dismiss it with a retrospective shudder. It was a command, direct, urgent and, above all, persistent. Nothing quite like it had ever befallen him.

It is true that in his boyhood he had been subject to what later he called his "inhibitions." He would suddenly find himself impelled to comply with some self-denying ordinance, but there was usually the fear of a specific penalty to enforce obedience. Thus, on one occasion, he became convinced that if he bought any caramels in March he would catch

scarlet-fever. And though his weekly shillings had each of
them burnt a big hole in his pocket, he had refrained from
indulging himself. It is true that he didn't catch scarlet-fever,
but any pleasure he might have felt in having escaped the
epidemic of that Easter-term was greatly lessened when he
found that the victims were not only regarded as heroes, but
had had a glorious time in the sanatorium, spending their
convalescence bird-nesting, making model boats and eating to
their fill.

Another time, the inward monitor said, "If you don't visit
cousin Mavis this afternoon you will die of lock-jaw before
Shrove Tuesday." It was during the Christmas holidays, and
he and his brothers and sister were being taken that afternoon
into Brighton to see the pantomime. Cousin Mavis was a
crotchety cripple, and a member of his parents' generation
rather than of his own. He didn't in the least wish to see her,
and notwithstanding the natural egotism of youth, he
couldn't help doubting whether she wished to see him. None
the less, he made a fantastic excuse about feeling bilious, lay
down till the party had left for the theatre and then cycled
through muddy and hilly lanes to the village in which Cousin
Mavis lived. She had no cake in the house and seemed to
grudge giving him tea, bread and butter and jam. She must
have thought it exceedingly odd when he begged her not to
tell his parents that he had been to see her. That evening he
heard that the pantomime had been thrilling beyond words.

By the time he left Oxford he had, as he thought, out-
grown this mental kink, and when he recollected it, would
describe it to you in fashionably Freudian terms. "I suppose,"
he would say, "it was set up by some sordid little episode in
childhood. Perhaps my nurse or the butler did something
humiliating to me. Or it may have been a precocious guilt-

complex. I wonder if I felt, deep down, that I ought to have
been one of the world's workers, turning a wheel in a dreary
factory and joining in community-singing when 'Shirkers'
Playtime' came round. Perhaps that was my penalty for belonging to what subversive writers call the 'comfortable class'
—in other words, the only class which has to make a permanent reduction in its standard of living every time there's
a war." At this point his political indignation would get the
better of his self-analysis. If you had pressed him, he would
have had to admit with shame that he still had in him an
overdeveloped tendency to superstition, which caused him,
for example, to study the calendar secretly so as to avoid
seeing the new moon through glass, and that when choosing
a new tie he might suddenly feel that the one which attracted
him most would bring him bad luck—with the result that he
would buy another one instead, probably of not quite the
right shade. These moments however, were mere wrinkles on
the silken surface of a happy life. The warning or premoni-
tion he had received about the Chelsea Cat belonged to a different order of psychical events.

As he bathed, shaved, breakfasted and dressed on that
morning of the Hooper-Hoade sale, he was confused, miserable and indignant. The inhibition was lodged firmly in his
mind, like a toothache in a tooth that is irretrievably decayed. Yet to forego the delight of acquiring the Chelsea Cat
(and all the prestige it would bring him as a collector) was
unthinkable. What would Mr. Rebus say? And what would
happen to him personally, if he let himself be swayed, at the
most inconvenient moments, by what could only be the
relic of a childish neurosis? He must conquer it at once, or it
would become a fixed habit and lead him prematurely into
the hideous vacillations of old age. "No," he said to himself,

"I will not give in. I shall go to the sale, and—" Here, as if old age were already upon him, he vacillated, and continued to vacillate till noon, when Henry, his servant, went out to get him a taxi. Then, to the outrage of his habitual sobriety, he took a nip of brandy.

Scotties' sale-room was crowded. Distinguished amateurs and all the best-known dealers jostled one another round the high table. Among them was Mr. Rebus, who, at his usual seat near the auctioneer's rostrum, was bending his lean, sensitive and swarthy face over a catalogue which he studied through half-closed lids. Yes, there was still time to pass him a note. "Dreadfully sorry, but I've changed my mind about the Chelsea Cat. Please don't bid more than £400 for me." That would be quite safe. It was bound to fetch at least double that price. In an agony of indecision, Mr. Mallowbourne twisted and turned at the back of the crowd.

Lot 98. This was the late Vienna coffee-service, for which he had arranged to make one or two small bids himself, so as to pay for his footing, as it were, and mislead the dealers into thinking that here lay his reason for coming to the sale. "Shall I start at £20?" the auctioneer asked. How quietly the bidding went—20, 22, 24, 26, 28. He must intervene, as soon as there was a pause. 38. Mr. Mallowbourne, who was tall, drew himself up and waved his catalogue. "Forty at the back," said the auctioneer, acknowledging the bid. 42, 45, 48. Mr. Mallowbourne shook his head and turned round, trying unsuccessfully to give the smile of one who accepts a crushing defeat with a good grace.

Lot 99, lot 100. Even now, he could pass a note to Mr. Rebus. He felt for his gold pencil and couldn't find it. He had left it at home, and had also forgotten to fill his fountain-pen, which he took out of his pocket and tried on a blank page in the catalogue. It wrote, very faintly, "I'm dreadfully sorry, but," and then ran completely dry. The rest was scratches. Lot 101. Suddenly he thought, "Perhaps I'm meant to have it after all!" The idea that we are *meant* to do things was not normally part of his philosophy, but much must be excused to him that morning. Lot 102. "And after all, why not?" Perhaps the Chelsea Cat would rid him for ever of his last vestige of superstition. Lot 103. His eyes strayed to the far end of the sale-room behind the auctioneer, where the objects for sale were brought up in systematic rotation before making the grand tour of the table. Yes, it was there, behind a pair of vases—fine vases, too, decorated with exotic birds, Worcester of the Dr. Wall period. Mr. Mallowbourne was delighted to find that he could appraise them with detachment. He wouldn't mind having them, *too*. Lot 104. The vases came to the front, an attendant carried them past the people seated at the table. It was a ritual performance, but of small practical significance; for all serious would-be purchasers had already examined them with minuteness, when they were on view two days before the sale. The bidding was high. Forgetting his qualms, Mr. Mallowbourne hoped that whoever was destined to be his competitor for the Cat would squander all his resources on the vases.

And now, lot 105—sitting plumply on the attendant's tray, a glossy porcelain cat, pure white except for its greenish-brown eyes, two spots of colour for the nostrils and a black ribbon round its fat neck. Its long tail curved round to the left, and its right paw was indolently raised in the air. You would have said—or rather, Mr. Mallowbourne would have said—that it had lived on a diet of cream and spiced mouse on toast. Then, with a burst of panic, all his anxieties returned. What was he doing? What act of madness was he committing?

He felt like one who dices with the devil. Was there no way of
halting the proceedings? Could he bring himself to shout, "I
disown any bid made by Mr. Rebus?" If only someone would
jog the attendant's arm as he carried the tray round. Or why
shouldn't the attendant have an attack of faintness? Did they
never drop things, break things? Mr. Mallowbourne had many
a bitter memory of his own housekeeper's breakages. There
was one almost every week—cream-jug, dessert-plate, teapot. (Mrs. Widdon must go, he decided.) Surely there
might, for once, be a breakage at Scotties'? It would be
such a simple solution.

£700. £740. £780. The representative of the Connaught
and Coburg Institute of Ceramic Art had fallen out now, and
the field was left to Mr. Rebus and a genial pug-faced little
man, who, Mr. Mallowbourne had heard, acted for some
American collectors and one or two American museums.
£1,000. £1,050. That was Mr. Rebus' bid. Go it America, go it
Pug-face! £1,100. Well done, indeed! £1,150. Oh dear, of
course that was Mr. Rebus. But it was his last chance. Now,
Pug-face, one more effort. Think how little it means to you
in dollars. Just one more bid, and Mr. Mallowbourne will
be saved. But Pug-face didn't make it. There was a dreadful
pause. The auctioneer raised his hammer, looked searchingly
round the room, gave a soft rap on his desk and announced,
slowly and quietly, "One thousand, one hundred and fifty
pounds. Mr. Rebus."

"And worth every penny of it, I should say, by present
standards." It was Mr. Vesperidis, who had taken Mr. Mallowbourne gently by the arm. Mr. Vesperidis was the grand
old man of the London dealers in porcelain. He had long
retired from active business, his faculties were not what they

had been, and he was often a bit of a bore, but people treated him with respectful indulgence and it was an honour to receive his confidences. "Do you know, Sir," he continued, "that piece once passed through my hands? It must have been forty, no, nearer fifty years ago when I sold it to Lord Innistartan. It was the last thing his lordship ever bought from me, or from anyone else. He was found three days later in his gun-room, shot through the head. They do say that no collector has ever sold or disposed of the Chelsea Cat. A splendid piece indeed. I wonder whom Rebus is acting for today."

Mr. Mallowbourne didn't enlighten him, but tottered out of the room, feeling slightly sick.

The Cat arrived the same evening, by special messenger. Mr. Mallowbourne unpacked it as though performing an unpleasant duty, gave it a close professional scrutiny to make sure it had sustained no damage in the sale-room or in transit, put it in his most prominent china-cabinet, in a position he had selected with wild anticipations of delight the evening before, shut the glass doors, locked them, wrote out his cheque and put the letter on the hall table for Henry to take to the post. "No one can say," he thought bitterly, "that I am not punctilious *to the last.*"

After dinner, at which he drank rather more Chateauneuf du Pape than was his habit, he felt more like his old self. Whatever was destined to happen he was now the owner of

the Chelsea Cat. It was an event in ceramic history. Perhaps
he ought to add a codicil to his Will, leaving the Cat to the
Connaught and Coburg. "Dear Atkinson, as I have recently
acquired an object of national importance, I feel it my duty
. . ." And insurance. That also must be dealt with. As for
Vesperidis' story, after all, the animal dated from the seventeen-fifties—the earlier seventeen-fifties, he liked to think—
and in the course of nearly two hundred years must have had
many owners. It would not be surprising if one of them had
come to a tragic end.

With an impulse of bravado, he unlocked the doors of the
cabinet, took out the Cat and ran his finger over the glaze.
"Dear Puss, dear Puss," he murmured, as he put it back and
shut and locked the doors.

He went to bed, pleasantly numb in mind and body. But
when, on the verge of sleep, he repeated that beautiful line
(from an imaginary poem)

Dear Puss shall purr me through a ripe old age . . .

it didn't sound quite convincing.

3

Next morning, when Henry was setting out breakfast on a
charming butterfly Pembroke table in Mr. Mallowbourne's
bedroom, he said, in his gossipy way, "I can't think what's become of Tompkins, Sir. He was out last night, visiting friends
in the square as usual, I suppose, but he hasn't come in this
morning. I've never known him late for breakfast before.
Well, I shall probably find him in the kitchen when I go downstairs."

Tompkins was the household cat, a tabby and an excellent

mouser. He was not encouraged above stairs, because claw-marks on a piece of Chippendale and one or two rents in the brocade of a wing-chair had been attributed to him, but Mr. Mallowbourne regarded him with a tolerant affection and never failed to caress him when they met.

"Dear me, Henry, this is most surprising. But surely Tompkins knows how to take care of himself by now. It isn't as if he were still a kitten. No doubt he'll be in later during the morning."

Then a most unpleasant thought occurred to him. Was Tompkins jealous or *frightened* of the new arrival?

Henry made diligent search in the little streets and alleys of the quiet neighbourhood without result. Mr. Mallowbourne himself went into the garden of the square and peered into the thick shrubberies, calling "Tompkins, Tompkins," but there was no answering miaow.

At about half past five Mrs. Widdon sent up word by Henry that she was feeling far too ill to cook dinner and had gone to bed. She didn't want to see a doctor. It was just another of her "turns," though a worse "turn" than usual. Mr. Mallowbourne dined badly at his club.

He sat for a long time after dinner, in the monumental coffee-room, reflecting gloomily. Surely it wasn't possible that he was to be the victim of ill-luck resulting from the ownership of an object endowed with malevolent powers. He had always regarded tales of amulets and scarabs inscribed with a curse as being no less nonsensical in fact than they were tedious in fiction. It was absurd to let himself be worried by Vesperidis' silly story. Whatever might have happened to Lord Innistartan, Hooper-Hoade had had the Cat in his collection for at least ten years. And nothing very dreadful

had happened to him. It was true that he had been killed in a
motor-accident, but so are many people, and it isn't really
one of the worst ways of dying. Was there anything else that
one had heard about him? Oh, of course, the first wife had
committed suicide. The balance of her mind was said to have
been disturbed by an air-raid. Probably that was quite true.
Then Mr. Mallowbourne uttered another and more pro-
longed "Oh" as he recalled the rumours about Hooper-
Hoade's three sons. The eldest had been involved in an un-
savoury matrimonial case with that notorious Biddowfield
woman. The second had received an even wider publicity
when he was warned off the Stock Exchange and the Turf.
And the third son, the good boy of the family and heir to
the business, had been killed in France on D-Day.

Mr. Mallowbourne gasped and rang for a brandy. Well,
somehow Hooper-Hoade had borne up in spite of these disas-
ters. He had even married again—but what a woman! Thirty-
five years younger than her husband and a good-for-nothing
gold-digger. It was said that she got a hundred thousand
pounds out of him before she ran away with somebody in a
dance-band. "Good riddance," Mr. Mallowbourne would
have said, but perhaps Hooper-Hoade didn't take the same
view. By the way, *was* it a verdict of accidental death that
they brought in after the motor-smash?

Mr. Mallowbourne hardly dared to go home, for fear that
he would be greeted by the news of some further calamity.

4
―――――

The next day Mrs. Widdon felt rather better and got up.
But she soon had to go back to bed, and Henry was sure she
ought to see a doctor. The trouble was, she had taken a dis-

like to her panel-doctor, who, she said, was rude to her, and she wouldn't have him sent for. Mr. Mallowbourne sighed. (All this insurance that we pay for other people.) Then he said, "Suppose I ask Dr. Cookwell to come round. Do you think she'd see him?" "Oh yes, Sir, I'm sure she would. She says Dr. Cookwell is such a nice gentleman."

Dr. Cookwell was Mr. Mallowbourne's own doctor and a friend as well. He collected French paper-weights, and was sufficiently interested in porcelain to be able to ask intelligent questions about it and listen attentively to the answers. He had a practical and optimistic temperament which Mr. Mallowbourne found exhilarating.

He called at half-past six, and when he had examined Mrs. Widdon, went to the big sitting-room on the first floor, to drink a glass of sherry with Mr. Mallowbourne. He looked a little more serious than usual and said, "I'm afraid she must go to hospital to be investigated properly. I think it's gall-bladder. Of course, I've every hope that we can put it right by dieting, and that she won't need an operation."

"Ought she to go at once?"

"Well, the sooner the better. I don't mean tonight, of course. These things take a bit of fixing up nowadays."

"You mustn't spare any reasonable expense. She's been with me quite a long time."

"That's very good of you. Can I use your telephone?"

During the conversation, Mr. Mallowbourne sat nervously sipping his sherry.

"Gall-bladder, did you say?" he asked when the doctor had finished. "You know, I've often been a bit worried about that, myself. Sometimes I get a pain just here; not a bad one *yet*—but—"

"Wind," said the doctor. "That isn't at all the place for a

gall-bladder pain. I say, is that something new?"

He pointed to the Chelsea Cat in the china-cabinet.

"New? I should think it is. I got it two days ago at Scotties'. It cost me a fortune and seems to have brought me nothing but trouble. Would you like to have a look at it?"

They studied it together for some time, while Mr. Mallowbourne gave one of his little lectures. But the doctor noticed that it was strangely lacking in gusto.

"If I were you," he said, "I should be so excited that I shouldn't know what to do. You sound almost as if you were depressed. You're not really worrying about your gall-bladder, are you? I tell you, yours is perfectly healthy. Well, I must be going now, as I have to be at the hospital by eight. If Mrs. Widdon gets any worse, let me know, and I'll come round at once. She should be feeling more comfortable tomorrow, if she does as I've told her. No, no, don't bother to come down with me."

5

An unhappy fortnight followed. Tompkins did not return. Mrs. Widdon was taken to hospital and replaced temporarily by two sisters. In addition to exceeding Mrs. Widdon's normal average of breakages, they so unsettled the charwoman who came to help in the mornings that she refused to do any more rough work. "She's willing to take on a dusting job," Henry reported, "but she says there aren't any charwomen nowadays. They call themselves 'Domestic Appliances' or some such name, and it means they won't scrub floors or carry coals." Mr. Mallowbourne thought ruefully how, only a few seconds before the Chelsea Cat became his, he had said to himself, "Mrs. Widdon must go."

But these pinpricks of irritation were of small importance compared with the feeling of uneasy tension which obsessed him throughout his waking hours. He went over Vesperidis' remarks again and again, and evolved from them a new superstition to the effect that if he sold the Cat, or even gave it away, his plight would be still graver than it was. And he was forced to admit to himself that both these possibilities had occurred to him.

One morning, after breakfast, when he went down as usual to the big sitting-room on the first floor, he noticed with horror that the Chelsea Cat had changed its position in the cabinet. It was now on the shelf below where it should have been, crowding out the Bow figures. For a moment the last vestige of skepticism left him, and he gazed at the sleek little animal as if it were a viper. Then he remembered that he had taken it out of the cabinet the previous night, and found a slender comfort in supposing that he must have put it back on the wrong shelf; though the thought that he could have been so absent-minded or unbalanced as to do such a thing was hardly reassuring. He wouldn't have cared to tell you why he had taken it out, but the truth was that he wished to examine it yet again in case it had any sinister or cabalistic inscription upon it. Needless to say, he found nothing except the small red anchor tucked discreetly by the tip of the tail. If there had been anything else, a dozen experts would have noticed it long ago, and the fact would have been mentioned in Scotties' catalogue and the two books in which the Cat had already been illustrated.

Using his concern over Mrs. Widdon as an excuse, he asked Dr. Cookwell if he could call and see him and stay to dinner. It was not till they were sitting over coffee that he could nerve himself to speak of his real troubles. He ex-

plained as lightly as he could, that on the very morning of
the sale he had had a superstitious feeling that the Chelsea Cat
would bring him bad luck, but that he had refused to give
way to it. He repeated what Vesperidis had said to him at the
sale, and gave an outline of the calamities which had dogged
—though *catted* might be a more appropriate verb—the un-
fortunate Hooper-Hoade. Then with a timid little laugh he
mentioned the Cat's change of position.

As always, his friend was full of robust common sense.
"What does it all boil down to?" he asked. "I know nothing
about Lord Innistartan, though I dare say this Vesperidis,
who you say is an old fool anyway, has got the story quite
wrong. As for Hooper-Hoade, the things that happened to
him are happening every day to big business-men. A neurotic
first wife, ne'er-do-well sons—it was sad about the youngest
one, but a good many people were killed on D-Day—and a
silly second marriage. What if the car-smash wasn't an accident? Big business-men are apt to commit suicide when
things go wrong. It suits their megalomania. And what about
you? Nothing very terrible has happened to you, has it? Your
nice cat has been stolen. That happened to my mother, twice.
And you've had some domestic worries. Who hasn't in these
days? As for your putting the Cat back on the wrong shelf,
your nerves are so much on edge that I wonder you didn't
drop it. If you're not very careful, I shall take it away myself
and sell it, and buy paper-weights with the money."

As the doctor spoke these words, a strange feeling of relief
passed quickly through Mr. Mallowbourne's mind. What a
wonderful deliverance that would be!

But the doctor went on, "If it comes to that, why don't *you*
sell it?" And Mr. Mallowbourne had to quote Vesperidis again

and explain that he felt himself destined, having bought the Cat, to keep it—and pay for its keep.

"I was thinking you might give it to the Connaught and Coburg, if you have scruples—probably just pride, really—about selling it. Then you'd double your prestige and get rid of your neurosis."

"No, I shouldn't. Besides, it would hardly be fair to the Connaught and Coburg. Heaven knows what might happen to the Institute and the Directors."

Dr. Cookwell sighed and looked at his watch. "Now you're being really silly," he said. "I'm afraid the thrill of being such a big noise in porcelain has unbalanced you. Never mind, you'll get over it. Now I must leave you, as I've still got some work to do tonight. Give me a ring if you don't feel much better in a few days."

Dr. Cookwell's "few days" went by and brought Mr. Mallowbourne no peace of mind. His mood alternated between a panicky apprehensiveness and the apathy of nervous exhaustion, while in his less self-centered moments he began to feel that he was morally responsible for Mrs. Widdon's illness, which had taken a disquieting turn. More often, however, he was alarmed about himself. Could this be the onset of one of those terrible and intractable nervous diseases about which he had vaguely heard? Was his reason in danger? A bitter thought for one who prided himself on the excellence of that faculty.

Yet in his home-life nothing untoward happened. Henry managed to replace the two sisters and the Domestic Appliance. Mr. Mallowbourne went to the sale-rooms as a self-discipline, but he shunned his fellow-collectors, and porcelain made him feel sick, particularly if it was an animal-figure.

The zest had gone out of his life. He hardly cared if there were to be a capital-levy or not. "I'll give myself till the end of the month," he decided. "If I'm no better by then, I'll telephone to Cookwell and ask him to take me to a specialist. This can't be allowed to go on."

Hardly had he made this heroic resolution, when, to his very great relief, the obsession became a little less constant. He found himself able to forget it for an hour or two at a time. He no longer fought quite so shy of his friends, and even accepted one or two invitations to quiet bachelor dinners. Perhaps after all, as Cookwell had suggested, the intense excitement of having become the Chelsea Cat's owner had been temporarily too much for his nervous system. Well, he would conquer the trouble by himself and show Cookwell that he wasn't so spineless as he must have appeared.

On the last night of the month he had an excellent dinner with an acquaintance who collected enamels. Mr. Mallowbourne, who would have liked to be a connoisseur of all the arts, listened appreciatively while his host explained the finer aspects of his hobby. After speaking of the numerous late nineteenth century fakes commonly offered for sale as Battersea or Bilston work, he said, "If I'd had to form my collection from the stuff displayed in the average shop-window, I shouldn't have got very far. Luckily, I knew Princess von Stuetzelburg well enough to be able to make her an offer for her husband's collection *en bloc*. Otherwise it would have gone to Scotties' with the other things, and been split up, and Americans would have out-bid me for most of it."

"Stuetzelburg?" said Mr. Mallowbourne. "Yes, I knew, of course, that he was a collector, but I never did see his things and I didn't really know there was ever a Stuetzelburg sale. I can't think how in the world I came to miss it."

"There wasn't a Stuetzelburg sale, at least in that name," his friend replied. "Perhaps I'm wrong to betray a confidence, but anyhow the Princess is dead now and there are none of the family left in England. And you needn't pass on what I'm going to tell you. You may remember that the Princess was a Belgian and had an estate in her own right, on the German frontier. Stuetzelburg and his wife spent most of the year in their huge flat in Park Lane, and that's where he kept his collections—at all events, his English collections. He was anti-Nazi and couldn't live in Germany under Hitler. He did however pay a visit to his wife's property in 1937—or it might have been early in 1938. He said he was going simply on business, but I think there must have been more to it than that. You know he enjoyed playing the part of a mystery-man, and he may have fancied himself in the role of the Scarlet Pimpernel. At any rate, he went to the Belgian estate, and either crossed the border into Germany or was kidnapped and dragged over it. He never came back. In due course the Princess had news of his death—news evidently authentic enough to satisfy the authorities over here. Like many of the international nobility, she had relations living in Germany, and it may have been for their sake that she put it about that her husband had been found dead in bed one morning from natural causes. The truth is that he had been tortured to death in a concentration camp. It's hard for us to believe that such things really happened, isn't it? The Princess was her husband's Executrix, though not his residuary legatee, and when she came to sell his things, she took every possible step to prevent people from knowing that they were his. I don't know whether it was family pride, or whether she was afraid of its getting about that he had owned so many precious things, but not only were the sales held anonymously—'Property of a Gentleman of Title' and so on —but she even went so far as to deny to people who had seen the actual objects in her husband's collections that he was the real owner. She would say, 'Oh, that wasn't *his*. He was only housing it for a friend.' I think that was why she accepted my offer for his enamels. It avoided publicity. By the way, do you remember that Chelsea Cat which was sold at Scotties' the other day—from the Hooper-Hoade collection? That was really one of Stuetzelburg's pieces. But even Hooper-Hoade didn't find out that when he bought it. He used to say, 'Somehow it came into the possession of a Parson in the Midlands.' The Parson in the Midlands was Prince Hugo von Stuetzelburg, who was cut up with razor-blades in a Bavarian concentration-camp. Oh, do have another whisky before you go."

6

When Mr. Mallowbourne reached home he was feeling far from well. And he felt still more unwell, when he went into his sitting room and saw that the Chelsea Cat had had kittens. Even in that moment of collapse, it occurred to him that there was something peculiarly disquieting and obscene in the idea that the Cat was a female. Such events don't go together. All cats, like many human beings, should be neuter. But there the kittens were, wriggling repulsively along the shelf, and it was only by making the greatest of efforts that he was able to keep his finger on the bell long enough to rouse Henry and say, "Get Dr. Cookwell at once, and tell him I'm very ill," before he fainted.

7

A hour later he was lying on a sofa in the sitting-room, with a glass of brandy on a table by his side.

Dr. Cookwell, who had listened to him patiently without saying very much in reply, asked suddenly, "Have you the key to that cabinet in your pocket?"

"Yes. Why?"

"I'd like to have a look at the Chelsea Cat, if you don't mind."

Mr. Mallowbourne turned his head apprehensively towards it, but there were no kittens there now.

"Here it is."

"Thanks." Dr. Cookwell unlocked the glazed doors, lifted out the Cat and turned it this way and that in the light of a standard-lamp by the fireplace. Then he took a handkerchief and wrapped it around the animal. Mr. Mallowbourne supposed that he was going to rub off any finger-marks he might have left on that immaculate surface and watched with a feeling of detachment. But instead of wiping the Cat, the doctor laid it, completely covered in the handkerchief, on the marble hearth-stone, picked up the coal-shovel and brought it down on the little bundle with a vigorous blow. There was a crash of breaking china. Then he knotted the ends of the handkerchief as if it contained an old-fashioned workman's lunch, and put it in his coat-pocket.

"This is going into the Thames tonight," he said. "It's done you quite enough harm. I'll ask Henry to see that you get safely to bed. I'll telephone tomorrow. Goodnight."

He rang the bell as if he were in his own house and went downstairs. Mr. Mallowbourne, hardly knowing if he was alive or not, heard him talking to Henry in the hall. Then the front door shut and the doctor drove away.

Mr. Mallowbourne spent the next morning in bed, reading Jane Austen. He felt weak, but agreeably convalescent and happy in himself. He got up after luncheon, and took a little walk. The lilacs in the square were just beginning to flower and there was a hint of summer in the air.

Shortly before dinner-time he rang up Dr. Cookwell, from whom he had heard nothing during the day. When he got no reply a vague uneasiness came over him, but he fought it down. He had done with all these worries for good and all.

8

On the following day he had a letter in his breakfast post from the senior partner of a firm of art publishers, whom he knew fairly well.

Dear Mallowbourne,

These things can't be kept hidden! I must indeed congratulate you on being the lucky owner of the Chelsea Cat. What does it feel like to be so celebrated?

The point of this letter is to tell you that we have got Mimpley of the Connaught and Coburg to write us a monograph on the *Cat in Porcelain*. The book will be published at 5 guineas and will have above 100 illustrations, 6 of which will be in colour. As yours is the senior English Cat, we should be very grateful if you would let us use it for the frontispiece. Needless to say, we shall ascribe it to your collection, unless you object.

By the way, I think the following will interest you. I was dining the other night with a man who goes in for eighteenth century engravings. He showed me some in a portfolio, by an artist called

Amos Bolberry, whose work I confess I hardly knew. One of them struck me at once. It depicted a sleek, contented white cat with a black ribbon round its neck, sitting in exactly the attitude of your cat—right paw raised, tail curled round to the left—in the foreground of a squalid and horrifying room. Two naked children lay dead on the floor, their arms round one another. A dead woman was drooping half out of a large bed, and beyond her was the husband with convulsed face and arms outstretched in a death-agony. In front of the foot of the bed was the writhing body of a youth. The picture was inscribed:

I LIVE IN A HOUSE OF DEATH.

This Bolberry, I was told, was fond of reproducing the work of earlier artists, especially that of an eccentric Yorkshireman named Samuel Hucks. We know that Hucks came as a young man to London from the north at the time of the Restoration of Charles II, and went about making sketches of what he saw in the great city. We know that he was in London during the great plague of 1665, and (to quote a 19th century critic) "delineated with a masterly skill those tragic and awful scenes of which he was so intrepid an eye-witness." To the best of my friend's knowledge the original drawing by Hucks, on which we presume Bolberry to have based his engraving, has not been found. But it is not only pleasant but reasonable to conjecture that Hucks did actually see a white cat living quite unperturbed "in a house of death," and made a drawing on the spot of what he saw. It would be quite in character that he should do so; for there is a vein of morbidity in all his work.

And now for something that may interest you still more. Bolberry dedicated a number of his engravings—though we cannot be sure that this engraving was among them—to Sir Everard Fawkener, whose connexion with the Chelsea factory in its early years is better known to you than to me.

Just a little more evidence, and we should have all the links in the chain—the original white cat sitting among the plague-stricken corpses, the inquisitive Hucks (who nowadays would have been a journalist with a camera), jotting down the details in his sketch-book, the reproduction of his drawing, some eighty years later, by Bolberry, and its dedication to Sir Everard Fawkener, who suggested to some modeller in the Chelsea factory that the Cat would be an effective subject.

Perhaps you would like to undertake the research, and write us an Appendix to the description of your figure. I know Mimpley would be quite happy about it, and the friend who showed me the Bolberry engraving would be delighted to show it to you and give you the benefit of his knowledge. No wonder your Cat is so precious. It must be almost the only instance, at that date, of a Chelsea production which owed nothing to Germany or the East and had a purely English origin. . . .

Mr. Mallowbourne dressed slowly, a prey to conflicting thoughts. His chance of becoming an immortal in the world of porcelain had been smashed to fragments in his own fire-place. There was a blank space in his china-cabinet and a big hole in his bank-account. And how was he to explain away what had happened? What a number of little lies he would have to tell to friends and dealers. ("Don't let Mallowbourne handle your things," they would say. "He drops them.") It was intolerable that such clumsiness should be imputed to him, yet it seemed hardly fair to let poor Cookwell take the blame. "Well, at any rate, no doubt it was fully insured," they would say. And he would have to equivocate once more; for naturally he could make no claim on the Insurance company.

And yet, how glorious it was to have recaptured his old serenity, to be at peace in himself and read Jane Austen, and walk about like a free man, enjoying the lilacs and cherries in the square.

He was busy with this two-fold meditation, when the front-door bell rang and Henry came up with a visiting-card.

"There's a Mr. Frenchford—a gentleman from the district Medical Officer of Health, would like to see you at once, Sir, if it's not inconvenient."

"Tell him there are no drains in *this* house—," Mr. Mallowbourne began, with indignant pomposity. Then a new and terrible thought struck him. "No, no. Please show Mr. Frenchford up at once."

Mr. Frenchford was a youngish man of pleasing manner and appearance.

"I am very sorry, Sir," he said, when Mr. Mallowbourne had asked him to sit down, "to be the bearer of some news that is bound to come as a shock to you. You are well acquainted, I believe, with a Dr. Cookwell?"

"Yes."

"In fact, Dr. Cookwell was here only the night before last, seeing you professionally?"

"Yes."

"Well, I'm afraid I must come to the point at once, Sir. Dr. Cookwell has been taken to the Isolation Hospital with what seems to suggest a very virulent form of small-pox, though some of the symptoms—"

"Are more like those of the great Plague of 1665," said Mr. Mallowbourne, unable to resist what was perhaps to be his last chance of creating a sensation.

Mr. Frenchford looked at him with astonished admiration.

"I must say, Sir, your guess is not so very wide of the mark. The disease was assumed to be small-pox, because Dr. Cookwell, who, as you probably know, does voluntary work two evenings a week at the Royal Thamesmouth Hospital, had been in contact with a patient, a coloured sailor, who was suspected of suffering from small-pox. It now seems that there's some doubt about the man's condition, but the fact remains that Dr. Cookwell is very dangerously ill, and it is our duty to seek out and warn all those with whom he has lately been in close contact, both for their own sake and the sake of the public. As you know, Sir, we have certain powers under Acts of Parliament, but we only use them in the very last resort."

"What would you like me to do?"

Mr. Frenchford told him.

Whatever forces of malevolence and evil there may have been in the white cat which watched the death of its owner and his family with quiet satisfaction in 1665, and whatever relics of those forces may have been transmitted through Hucks' drawing and Bolberry's engraving, to the porcelain figure modelled at Chelsea during the Red Anchor period, they fought a losing battle against those twin good fairies of modern bio-chemistry, Metaviolin and Pianofortinol.

Dr. Cookwell made a quick and complete recovery. Mr. Mallowbourne, who spent an anxious, but somehow not altogether unhappy fortnight at the Isolation Hospital, never showed any signs of catching the disease, and when he returned home (having been warmly complimented by the authorities on his public-spirited and prudent co-operation with them), he had the news that Mrs. Widdon would soon be rejoining his household in full health.

He has sold all his porcelain, and is now collecting French gold boxes of the reigns of Louis XIV and XV. The only piece of china, apart from domestic wares, in his house, is an unimportant little Rockingham figure of a brown tabby, which he keeps in memory of Tompkins.

21.

Cat's Meat

ANON.

You, who've rejected the pick of the dish
   And flatly refuse to be stirred
By the mention of meat if you know there is fish
   Or of fish if you know there is bird,
Who insist on your sole being *a la bonne femme*
   And your chicken direct from the breast,
Who will only touch trout that has recently come
   From the shadowy shoals of the Test,
You who drink nothing that isn't Grade A
   And would turn up your nose at a mouse,
Whom I've actually seen moving coldly away
   From an underhung portion of grouse.
You who will listlessly trifle and toy
   With a dream of a cod kedgeree,
Are eating with every appearance of joy
   A very decayed bumble bee.

22.

The Spy

by MARIO BRAND

Mario Brand, a resident of sunny California, is the author of the short fantasy with which we bring our basket of cat tales to a close. In "The Spy" he provides an amusing and improbable answer to a question frequently posed to tomcats returning home from a night on the town—a question which Tequila himself, had he been asked, would not have been able to answer.

T<small>EQUILA</small> did not even stop to ponder his surroundings, or how he had gotten where he was. His four paws instinctively padded his eager body helter-skelter to the little doorway from which the overpowering waves of enticing catnip-smell emanated. He butted his sleek head through the diaphragm over the opening and when his head emerged on the other side, he found himself staring uncomprehendingly at a bright moving circle of light. Before he could look away, the light became feline heaven.

He embarked on a night of adventure in which he exchanged amorous experiences with friendly tabbies, gorged himself on luscious piles of fresh red meat, lapped at convenient bowls of rich warm milk and buried himself ecstatically in bewitching hills of fresh, moist catnip.

Nard, socio-psychological analyst, Grade II, watched from behind a viewscreen as Tequila emerged from the culvert-size integrator and crossed the small open space of the chamber leading to the catnip-baited door. The tomcat's head hardly entered the hypno-chamber before he had expertly injected the now-immobilized animal with a modified form of Insulin. Satisfied, he stepped back to make room for Casan, who was soon busily adjusting many complicated image-probes, blood analyzers and cerebral stimulators to the head and body of the entranced Tequila.

"You know," Nard observed, as Casan was placing the final probes in position, "I've often wondered if the molecular dissolution of a body on another planet and its trip here for reintegration alters any of its memory-images? After all, Earth is a million and a half light-years away. Quite a little distance!"

"I wouldn't worry about it," grunted Casan, crossly. He wrinkled his nose in disapproval at the penetrating odor of perfume which arose apparently from behind the cat's ears.

"Earthlings!" he exclaimed. "I suppose the female playfully daubed some of her odor-cover on their pet. We'll see in a few moments anyway, as soon as the Insulin has reduced the glucose level sufficiently."

"Oh, yes, to get back to what you said a few minutes ago— I don't think the Seidler Beam alters any memory-images at all. We've been using it for many centuries already and our information on Earth's technological progress keeps rolling in steadily. Just remember"—he gestured for emphasis— "during that period of time we've been using generations of

Earth cats as observers. They've lived right with the Earthlings ever since there has been any social structure there
worthy of the name. Anyway, by correlating all the information from many observers we've been able to rule out any
errors that may have been made by any one observer because the individual error, or, for that matter, any memory-
image which may have been changed in the Beam's time-
ways, would show up as an inconsistency when we correlate
our final facts to show the whole event in question."

At this moment, a warning buzzer sounded to indicate
that the glucose level in the cat's blood was lowered as far
as the measured dose of Insulin was designed to take it.
Casan energized the cerebral probes and adjusted the re-
corder. On a small monitor screen in the main unit's master
panel there emerged a scene on Earth, as it had been seen
through the cat's eyes. The scene occurred five days ago.

"He must be on a chair," Nard pointed out, referring to
Tequila's position at the time.

"There! The floor just bounced up to cover the screen,
which indicates that he's jumped down from the chair.
There's a table leg approaching—he must be going to rub
against it."

Casan yawned. "Tell you what; I'm tired! I've read the
reports on this observer before and all we're really interested
in is a room called a 'Study' in this house. The cat's owner is
an engineer and his notes are on their rudimentary research
into quite simple problems of heat-exchange. If the observer
happens to wander into the Study, call my room and hold a
visiphone on the monitor screen. I'd like to see what further
notes the engineer has made; if any."

Nard agreed and returned to watching the many dials and

gauges that mirrored the mental and physical condition of the hypnotized cat. It was a monotonous vigil but he knew he was not alone. In thousands of rooms just like this one, all over the third planet of Almach, thousands of other analysts, like himself, were performing the same duties—observing, recording and monitoring thousands of Earth cats who had innocently and full of curiosity crawled into culverts and other small openings on Earth. Only the openings led into disintegrators, connected directly to Seidler Beam projectors which transported the cats instantaneously to the integrators on this planet.

Cats had been chosen by Nard's ancestors as admirable observers of the progress of Earth's science. The animals were extremely independent and thus they saw things and events objectively, devoid of the emotional overtones that usually distort observed reality. It was realized that cats were also the most curious of Earth animals and thus they prowled and investigated every nook and cranny of their planet. They chased mice out of university buildings housing cyclotrons as well as out of warehouses storing equipment for man's thus far feeble attempts to overcome his planet's imprisoning gravity.

Cats had been the close companions of Earth's leading scientists and mathematicians and had solemnly listened to lectures and explanations of problems which could better be worked out by verbalizing—especially to an intelligent audience such as the silent, attentive, and appreciative house pet.

The original choice of cats had been one of necessity as the primitive Seidler Beams could not handle too large a burden over such a distance. But, by the time the beaming apparatus was refined sufficiently to where larger objects

could be transported, the cats had become indispensable and trusted observers. It was generally agreed that they would remain in that capacity.

As Tequila's glucose level began rising to normal again and as inactivated brain cells gradually returned to use, Tequila relived his experiences of the last five days. That is, his unconscious relived them. His consciousness was blissfully hypnotized to where the pleasure-principle reigned supreme. The memory-images indelibly impressed on his brain cells were reviewed, painstakingly recorded and evaluated for whatever new information might be revealed.

Nard hastily dialed Casan's apartment two hours later as he saw the Study approaching on the screen; which indicated Tequila was getting ready to prowl the room. A sleepy Casan answered but he was soon alert when he saw the screen on his visiphone.

Tequila cautiously entered the room and slowly surveyed it for signs of occupants. Finding none, he approached a window and luxuriously, but illegally, sharpened his claws on the enticing draperies. Then springing lightly up on a table he sniffed at the books and the lamp in the center.

Casan saw the titles and grimaced; Science Fiction, no doubt! Earthlings had good imagination but their science lagged so far behind their ideas. Just goes to demonstrate how a primitive preoccupation with war and aggression can keep a ninth-class race from advancing to full acceptance in civilized Galactic society! He hoped this would take place soon for then the vigil of Earth would be over, although he had to admit that he was starting to like the four-footed observers and their individual bag of tricks.

Tequila, apparently bored with sniffing the table, glanced around the room again and his eyes lighted on the paper-cluttered desk. In an effortless leap he landed in the middle of the notes. With reckless abandon he batted an offending eraser to the floor and a letter, with its fold sticking tantalizing into the air, received like treatment.

Casan groaned for he had not had time to read its contents but saw that the letterhead was from a scientist-associate of Tequila's master. He made a note to examine each frame of the film being made to see if maybe one of them contained a full shot of the letter before it joined the eraser on the floor. However, the cat obligingly spent considerable time on the desk and Casan was able to read nearly everything lying on its top. Tequila even helped out some by engaging in a mock-battle with the papers and thus scattering some of the top layer onto the floor, revealing the notes underneath to Casan's view.

Suddenly the cat jumped to the floor, ran into the kitchen and then through a hinged affair in the door to the yard outside. Somebody no doubt was approaching and the shrewd pet had decided to leave the scene.

"That's about it!" Nard interrupted. "Glucose is back to normal and that's all we'll get this time. I'm going to get him ready for the trip back."

With that, he broke the connection as the screen showed Tequila approaching the culvert which contained the disguised Beam apparatus. The cat's memories over the last few days had been duly reviewed and recorded.

Nard quickly removed the probes and the other apparatus which had been utilized. The hypnotized cat was given a posthypnotic suggestion to awaken after one hundred fifty heartbeats and to remember only the pleasant dreams he had experienced. In one hundred forty-five cat-heartbeats Tequila traversed the Seidler Beam and on exactly the one hundred fiftieth he awoke in the same culvert he had entered a few hours ago.

It was nearly daybreak when Tequila finally butted through his private doorway cut in the kitchen door. The young couple with whom he deigned to reside were already seated at early breakfast and as the woman saw his entrance she frowned at him in puzzlement.

"Al," she addressed her husband's head over the morning paper, "where in Heaven's name do you suppose Tequila goes when he's out all night like that?"

About the Editor

Barbara Silverberg is a physicist presently doing research as a bio-medical engineer. She and her husband, Robert, a free-lance writer, have a large home in New York City, which they share with a varying number of cats, and a much larger number of books. When she is not involved in engineering, Mrs. Silverberg enjoys cooking and eating exotic foods, gardening, sewing, and traveling with her husband to far-off lands. Many of the photographs she has taken on these trips have later appeared as illustrations in her husband's books, but *Kitten Caboodle* is her first literary venture on her own.

About the Book

The text typeface is Linotype Granjon and the display typeface is Monotype Deepdene Italic. The book was printed by offset. Illustrations were done by the French artist, T. A. Steinlen, who was well-known for his posters and lithographs. Mr. Steinlen was born in Switzerland, but settled in Paris, where he lived until his death in 1923. Book designed by Hilda Scott.